WAIT FOR ME

BOOKS BY JAN THOMPSON

Protector Sweethearts (6 Books)
JanThompson.com/protector

Defender Sweethearts (6 Books)
JanThompson.com/defender

Binary Hackers (4 Books)
JanThompson.com/binary

Seaside Chapel (6 Books)
JanThompson.com/seaside

Savannah Sweethearts (11 Books)
JanThompson.com/savannah

Vacation Sweethearts (8 Books)
JanThompson.com/vacation

Keep up with Jan Thompson's book news:
JanThompson.com/newsletter

WAIT FOR ME

VACATION SWEETHEARTS BOOK 3

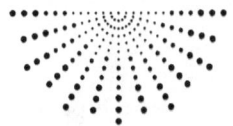

JAN THOMPSON

GEORGIA
PRESS

WAIT FOR ME (VACATION SWEETHEARTS BOOK 3)

First eBook Edition: September 2019
eBook ISBN 978-1-944188-31-3

First Paperback Edition: September 2019
Paperback ISBN 978-1-944188-32-0

To my Lord and Savior, Jesus Christ, who died on the cross to save me from my sins and rose again from the grave to give me eternal life in heaven.

For God so loved the world that He gave His only begotten Son, that whoever believes in Him should not perish but have everlasting life.
—John 3:16

READ THE VACATION SWEETHEARTS PREQUEL FOR FREE

When art gallery archivist Sheryl Breckenridge tries to get world-famous sculptor Winton Pace to display his artwork at Simon's Gallery, she doesn't expect him to fall in love with her. Will she reciprocate in this friends-to-more romance?

Read *Time for Me* (A Vacation Sweethearts Prequel) for FREE at the link below. This story starts thirteen months before *Smile for Me* (Vacation Sweethearts Book 1).

Download the FREE prequel here:
JanThompson.com/time-free

Sign up for Jan Thompson's mailing list to keep up with her book news. She writes Christian beach romance, romantic suspense, and suspense thrillers.

Subscribe to Jan's book news:
JanThompson.com/newsletter

ABOUT WAIT FOR ME

Their marriage didn't last.
The last thing he wants is to relive it.

A divorced single dad with full custody of his son made a promise he now has to keep: invite his ex-wife to enjoy their son's birthday gift: a seven-day cruise in Alaska. Can two people who have given up on each other put aside their emotions to make their five-year-old son happy for a week? What could possibly go wrong in this Christian romance with a sidearm of suspense?

LOVE HAS LEFT HIM...

Successful businessman Logan Urquhart regrets promising Jonas that he will give him anything he wants for his fifth birthday. The fortune he has inherited enables him to buy whatever his son desires. But all Jonas wants for his birthday is to be with his mother. "Dad, you promised."

Logan has no choice. Then again, it can't be too bad. It will only be for seven days. After that, he'll go home to Atlanta, Georgia, USA, and she'll go home to Paris, France. End of story. Or is it?

LOVE HAS RETURNED...

Undercover INTERPOL agent Marie Bouchard would love to see her son again, but not her ex-husband. Their lack of trust for each other destroyed their marriage three years ago. When he asked for a divorce, she gave him everything, including their son.

Well, the reunion will only be for one week. The problems that have followed her around for the last three years are all in the past, aren't they?

BUT LOVE IS TROUBLE...

All seem peaceful, until Marie notices extra security on board the ship. When her ex-husband becomes slightly paranoid about their son's safety, Marie begins to wonder if it is a mistake for her to be on board the cruise ship in the first place.

Wait for Me is the the third novel in *USA Today* Bestselling author Jan Thompson's Vacation Sweethearts Christian travel romance series celebrating the immeasurable grace and undeserved mercy of God. These novels are a spin-off of her Savannah Sweethearts beach romance series. Some of the novels in Vacation Sweethearts are also a prelude to the Protector Sweethearts Christian romantic suspense series.

Wait for Me (Vacation Sweethearts Book 3):
JanThompson.com/wait

Vacation Sweethearts:
JanThompson.com/vacation

Subscribe to Jan's Mailing List for Book News:
JanThompson.com/newsletter

WAIT FOR ME

PROLOGUE

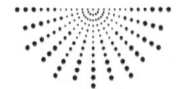

*L*ogan Urquhart regretted ever promising little Jonas that he would give him anything for his fifth birthday.

The fortune he had inherited enabled him to buy whatever his son wanted, including a whole toy store chain, pony rides to last a lifetime, and entire schools he would attend all the way through university.

But.

All Jonas Urquhart wanted for his birthday was to see his mom.

"Dad, you promised."

Logan stared at his beloved son sitting next to him at their dining table by the window that opened to a pleasant spring in metropolitan Atlanta.

They were eating peanut butter and jelly sandwiches, Jonas's favorite food, and drinking lemonade, also Jonas's favorite.

The little boy looked lonely.

Sometimes Logan wished he could give Jonas a sibling to play with.

In order to do that, Logan would need a wife. And he had no time for marriage—or remarriage— at this point in his life.

Jonas chewed his PBJ.

The silence between them broke Logan's heart.

He remembered when he had been very young, growing up as an only child of absentee parents, and only having his cousin Jared to call and talk to.

He remembered having prayed for years that God would give him a sibling. When God hadn't answered his prayer, Logan had turned his back against God.

It hadn't been until his college years at business school that he had realized how foolish it was for him to ignore God when the book of Proverbs was a fount of wisdom, which could be a blessing for Logan in his business.

As Logan looked at his son, he wondered what

kind of life Jonas would live, where he'd go, what he'd do so many years from now.

Would he recall this moment when his own dad had all but reneged on his promise to give his son whatever he wanted for his fifth birthday?

Logan sighed.

Yes, Logan Urquhart, the financial genius who, with his cousin Jared, ran the multibillion-dollar Urquhart Enterprises investment firm, had lost the battle to an almost five-year-old.

Thanks to his only son—to whom he had rarely refused—Logan must face Marie again.

Has it been three years since our divorce?

Logan didn't know the real reason he had married Marie. Deep down, he wondered if Marie had been right about their relationship, how it hadn't been based on any deep foundation.

They had met at a business conference in the French Riviera shortly after he and his first fiancée had broken up, six years ago now. Logan was smitten with Marie's charms immediately. The fact that she also spoke seven languages amazed him, and he hired the translator on the spot to accompany him and his cousin Jared to Sweden, where Urquhart Enterprises were to have a meeting with a Saudi businessman.

Her FBI background checks panned out. She

was a French translator who spoke English beautifully, almost like poetry. Within three months, Logan had proposed, and she had said yes. A lovely wedding on Cumberland Island, Georgia, sealed their love for each other.

Unfortunately, once they returned to Atlanta after Marie had applied for permanent residency, she grew antsy staying in the ten-bedroom house on Paces Ferry Road with nothing to do but pace the floor. Logan was gone all the time on business trips, and his paranoia that his pregnant wife should not fly—you know, all that radiation in the sky—Marie couldn't take it anymore.

Perhaps that had been why their marriage had lasted for only three years. By then, Jonas was almost two years old, and still needed his mommy. Marie intended to take him home with her to Marseilles, but there was no way Logan was going to let his American son leave the country.

Through the wit and tact of his family attorney, Logan had managed to wrestle the baby from Marie. Marie traveled for a living, the custody attorney had explained in court. She lived from hotel to hotel, job to job, embassy to embassy. Such was the life of a freelance translator much sought after by state departments and governments.

Who was going to watch the one-year-old while Marie went to work?

Instead of leaving him with nannies and strangers when he wasn't with his French grandparents, Marie had agreed to let Logan have full custody of Jonas.

Looking back, Logan wondered why Marie hadn't put on a fiercer fight. Maybe it was true that not only did Marie want out of the marriage, she also did not want to be reminded of Logan at all, as their son would certainly do.

Three years of single parenting later, Logan considered himself an expert at handling his son. Yet, there he was, bottom lip out, eyes on the verge of tears.

"All right," Logan found himself saying. "We'll fly to France for your birthday."

"Fly? No, Dad. I want to go on a big boat!"

"A ship?" Logan shouldn't have suggested that. He cringed.

"Yes, a ship!" Jonas clapped his hands and nodded his head, his blondish hair reminding Logan of Marie. "Can you buy me a ship, Daddy?"

"Not the one you want to go on." Logan wasn't sure if the kid understood.

"I want a ship!"

Does he have to shout out everything?

Logan tried to calm him down, but the boy had a big smile on his face. It was Marie's smile.

Melted Logan every time.

"Can we have my birthday on a ship?" Jonas asked. "Please?"

"Logistically, no. Don't you want all your friends to come to your birthday party?" Logan didn't feel like sending twenty or more kids and their parents or guardians on cruise just to eat a birthday cake.

"What's *jickally*, Daddy?"

No point explaining. "Why don't we celebrate your birthday first? Let's have a party here at home. We can have it outside in the playground, if you want. You can invite everyone in your kindergarten class, plus all your junior golf buddies and Sunday School class friends from church. After that, we can have a second birthday celebration on a ship just by ourselves."

Logan was thinking that a three- or four-day cruise in the Caribbean would do it. It was about as long as he'd wanted to be away from his office. So much work to do.

"With Mommy! Will she bring me presents?"

Presents. Plural. Never just one present. It has to be more and more.

What have I done with this kid?

"Uh, I'm sure she will."

Although Marie hadn't seen Jonas in these three years since she had left the United States, Logan didn't want Jonas to think that she had ignored him. If he had to give him a good memory, he would wrap up some presents and address it from Marie. She wouldn't mind, would she? After all, they always bought what the kid wanted.

"Woweee!" Jonas jumped up and down. "I want to see whales! And geezers!"

Logan coughed, suddenly feeling older than thirty-five years. "You mean glaciers?"

"Uh-huh. And bears and salmons... Dad, do they have eagles there?"

There was only one place in the world Logan could think of where they could see bears, salmons, eagles, whales, and glaciers in the same area.

Alaska.

He didn't want to go back there, really, to the place where he had proposed to Marie.

When was that?

He couldn't think of the date.

"Daddy, please?" Jonas tugged at his hand, smearing peanut butter—and probably saliva—all over it.

Logan stared at his son.

Well, he'd done it this time.

He had promised, and he must now deliver.

Logan had never broken any promise in his adult life, including his marriage vow. He was free and clear, blameless in every way.

The only relative in town, cousin Jared, had questioned Logan after the latter had signed the divorce papers, but Logan's conscience had been and was still now clear.

It pained Logan to recall that sad episode in his life. It had been as if someone had died.

What on earth had happened to their marriage?

Well, yeah, I wasn't about to learn any of the languages she knows, since she speaks flawless English, but surely it was more than that?

What had been so irreconcilable about his daily quarrels with Marie that had led to the abrupt end of their love story?

Funny. Logan couldn't remember the details of their arguments, only his own conclusions.

And he knew he didn't want Marie back in his life.

Not ever.

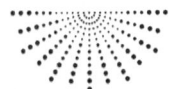

CHAPTER ONE

*M*arie Bouchard blamed herself for being absent from her son's life the last three years, even though there had been no way for her to call from deep undercover, not when the lives of her team members had been at stake.

Ironically, she had been in the Great Smoky Mountains in Tennessee back in October of the year before. It had been an FBI operation, although INTERPOL helped with the intel on the European side and Marie was embedded with the Americans since she could blend in with her American accent.

Deep undercover with FBI Special Agent Jake Kessler, Marie's job was to intercept everything said in French and translate that for Jake. After the operation was over, she was whisked out of the United States under the cover of night and flown home to Europe for their high-level debriefing in Lyon, France. Some higher-up bureaucrats didn't like the way the operation had gone, and caused Marie to be dismissed from the rest of the operation.

The very next day, Marie was reassigned to the French Riviera, where she began translating French into English for a British businessman whom the INTERPOL was very interested in. The French Riviera was exactly where Marie and Logan Urquhart had first met six years ago. There were so many memories there that she could barely focus on her job. On top of all that, chasing down a small-time drug trafficker was a demotion for her.

Yep. The last nine months had been nothing but a concerto of failures. For five years, they had failed to catch the fugitive of all fugitives, Molyneux. They failed to infiltrate her inner circle. What would it take to bring down the most notorious anarchist activist in the history of the world?

Certainly, taking seven days off to bask in the Alaskan sun and stare at glaciers and mountains was not Marie's idea of action.

It's unfair!

This vacation was forced on me! I didn't ask for it. But—

"Mommy!"

The high-pitched choir boy scream could slice off everyone's ears in the massive embarkation hall where thousands of passengers waited to board the *Alaskan Queen of the Arctic Seas.*

A fancy name for a refurbished 1969 cruise ship.

Marie's eyes darted back and forth from face to face in the sea of strangers, looking for something out of place—

"Mommy!"

Ah. Reality check.

I'm not at work.

No. I'm far, far away from my job. A whole continent away.

Far away from Vienna, where INTERPOL and the FBI were still digging through the ashes for clues, picking up the pieces of the damage left by Molyneux.

Marie caught herself.

Why am I thinking of Molyneux every waking hour?

She is not God.

Marie felt that she had to find Molyneux, who had destroyed the life of very good friend of hers,

Esperanza Diaz-Mendenhall, who had started out in Spain's Centro Nacional de Inteligencia. Esperanza had told Marie that if she helped her track down Molyneux, then she could stay at her mountain retreat for free the rest of her life.

Just what I need.

Another vacation.

"Mommy!"

Marie stared at her boy—little no longer—making his way through the crowd toward her, dragging his nanny with him.

How was he able to spot her in the crowd?

Sure, she was tall—nearly six feet—but there were many people in this hall.

Instinctively, Marie walked toward her son.

Behind him, his nanny repeatedly said, "Walk, walk. No running!"

But just like his dad, Jonas didn't listen.

Ah. I must be tired.

Marie chided herself for projecting upon this boy everything she had disliked about his father. Their pride had driven them apart, but primarily it had been Logan's inability to trust her.

He had wanted to know everything she did.

She could tell him absolutely nothing.

All she wanted him to do was trust her.

That, he couldn't do without full disclosure.

Marie stepped forward, the pain in her healing collar bones starting to bother her again. She could barely recall the raid two weeks ago now. All she could remember was her own sadness afterwards, when she had arrived at her apartment to take a hot bath and noticed the new email from Logan asking her to join them on an Alaskan cruise.

It was then that she realized she hadn't remembered her own son's birthday until Logan said so in his email. In fact, half his birthday celebration would be over before this cruise. His one-hundred-guest birthday party in the backyard of his house in Atlanta had been the highlight of the week. That could have been enough, Marie thought.

No. Jonas wanted more.

And Daddy would give him the world.

Jonas broke free from his nanny's grip, and flew into Marie, wrapping his arms around her waist so tightly that she could hardly breathe. His blond head, which he had inherited from her, came up to her abdomen.

He was so tiny when I left him with his dad...

Marie blinked.

Her motherly heart constricted.

How could I have left him?

She expelled her breath.

I had no choice.

"Miss Marie!" The nanny panted, catching her breath.

Miss Marie?

Miss Divorced Marie is who I am.

"Mrs. Ping, how are you?" Marie replied evenly.

Compartmentalize.

Her real name was Amanda Ping, but everyone called her Mrs. Ping. The fifty-five-year-old live-in nanny had been widowed for six years before Marie hired her.

Mrs. Ping had an interesting background that made her more of a bodyguard than a nanny. However, by the time Marie and Logan met her, she had retired from her past life and was running a dry cleaning business in metro Atlanta with her husband.

Soon, all her children had grown and moved away, and she was unable to run the dry cleaner by herself without her husband. Her children refused to help. Consequently, the business folded, and Logan took his suits elsewhere, but not before Marie hired Mrs. Ping to be Jonas's full-time nanny.

Eventually, Mrs. Ping stayed, while Marie lost her job as mommy.

Or had she?

Once a mother, always a mother, right?

"Mommy, I'm so happy you came." Jonas's voice was muffled in Marie's blouse, but she could hear him. "Please don't leave me again."

Was that a plea?

Someday, when Jonas grew up—if Marie was still alive—she would sit down with him over a cup of tea and explain everything to him.

She would hold nothing back, unlike what she had to do with Logan.

I had no choice.

CHAPTER TWO

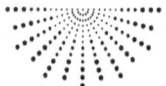

*O*nboard the *Alaskan Queen of the Arctic Seas*, their lunch was served buffet-style. Jonas was too excited to eat. Antsy and unable to sit down, he wanted to explore the children's activity center.

That sounded way too boring for Marie, so she let Mrs. Ping take Jonas.

As she sat alone by the window in the lunchroom, Marie wondered about her one-piece carry-on luggage that the stewards were taking taking to her stateroom at this moment. There wasn't anything in it save for her clothes, toiletries, and her books to be read, but still...

Then again, she had talked to the captain before coming to this deck for lunch.

Nothing to worry about, really.

She told herself that several times. It didn't help. She felt naked without her favorite Sig Sauer handgun. The sidearm was already in the safe in her stateroom. The captain of the ship knew who she was and why she carried it with her.

So much for this vacation.

She stared at the plate in front of her, at the calamari, mixed vegetables, stir-fried beef, and toast with strawberry jam, all huddling for space.

What in the world did I put on my plate?

It must be the jet lag.

She hadn't eaten anything since she had flown out of Lyon to Seattle by way of Paris and San Francisco. It had been a long flight, but the only one she could get.

And Logan had paid for her plane tickets.

As he had also paid for the three upper deck balcony suite staterooms they were staying in for seven nights. He had given her some privacy, but had put Mrs. Ping in the same stateroom as Jonas.

Must be nice to push off the caring of his son to a nanny...

Wait a minute. Didn't I have a part in it by moving out of the country without my son?

Her faced warmed at her own realization that she was a bona fide hypocrite.

This was truly an opportunity from God for her broken family to come together for seven days to take a normal family vacation—if it could be normal with all of them staying in separate staterooms.

Still, that space helped.

Helped what?

Marie pushed away the plate of food. She couldn't eat it. It wasn't that the international buffet she had absentmindedly piled on her plate looked simply inedible. It wasn't that she had been forced into a vacation by a five-year-old spitting image of his father.

The man she had once loved.

Marie looked up, wondering whether to get another plate and force herself to eat something to settle her nervous stomach.

Nervous?

She was rarely nervous, except...

Except when she was with Logan.

But he isn't here, is he?

He was probably in his stateroom conducting business calls and working on his vacation—

Nope. There he is.

Standing by the dessert bar, Logan towered over the petite woman dressed in the shortest mini skirt that Marie had ever seen. Shorter than a tennis skirt, for sure.

She was cute.

Logan seemed animated, telling a story, being lively and funny, as per usual—except during their last days of marriage together when he wouldn't even smile at her. Then, he had only laughed when he wasn't with Marie. Wouldn't that be considered a cruel and unusual punishment?

Now he laughed heartily with that little woman.

Marie tried to look outside the window next to her table. Grey, overcast skies the color of everyday Seattle went along nicely with her mood right now. Over the water, in the distance at the wharf, giant cranes stood still, waiting for their next call to labor.

Maybe it would be sunny, for a change, the next time she came to town—if there was ever another reason to visit Seattle than to settle into the gloom of a loveless marriage that once was.

She remembered their last cruise together—just Logan and her—sailing through the Aegean Sea in their attempt to resuscitate a dead marriage. They had fought for two days onboard that yacht. By the third day, they both had gotten off at Mykonos, and went their separate ways, the rest of the paid cruise drowned in the Mediterranean. Marie flew to her mother's house in Marseilles, and the next day, she filed for a divorce.

All that time, Jonas had stayed behind in Atlanta with his doting nanny.

Ah, dark days indeed.

Why am I thinking about the past?

Shouldn't I give it to God?

Why couldn't she compartmentalize this part of her life like she had compartmentalized different aspects of her career, playing roles in deep under-cover, taking on criminals all over the world, living her life as ordinarily as possible?

But she could not put her ex-husband away. Thoughts of him, memories of him, times with him had all persistently occupied Marie's mind for the last three years. No matter where she had been, what she had done, he had followed her around in her head.

And now, after three years, they had to confront each other again.

What was she going to say to him when they were together?

What was he going to say to her?

Here he comes.

Ah, she needn't have worried.

In what seemed like a great show of hatred for her, Logan walked past without even looking at her, registering a look of disgust that Marie had been familiar with.

Marie didn't turn to see where he was sitting, but she had seen enough. That scorn on his face had told her everything.

That's how he still feels about me.

CHAPTER THREE

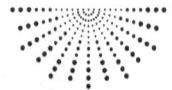

I probably shouldn't have done that.
And that other thing too.

Logan entered his stateroom, and made his way through the roomy space. He passed by his suitcase in the walk-in closet. He would unpack his clothes later, but at this time—even though it was Saturday —he had some business decisions to make.

His cousin, Jared, wanted Urquhart Enterprises—the family business they had inherited from their parents—to invest in a steel company in India. That New Delhi company was doing well, which meant a steady income for its investors.

But.

Jared himself was a partner in yet another company, Ruttledge Yamada Urquhart Commercial Properties, based out of Atlanta, but with branch offices in Savannah and on St. Simon's Island on the Georgia coast. He was stretched thin developing several mixed-use properties in those two coastal locations. The real estate projects had required Urquhart Enterprises to dip into their venture capitalist funds a bit too frequently.

And now, Jared wanted to add one more investment to their portfolio.

The way Logan looked at it, he wasn't sure their bank account could sustain one more investment, its future projected income notwithstanding.

Logan didn't have peace about it. He had told Jared he needed more time to pray about this.

God had worked it out for him in an interesting way. Jonas's birthday meant Logan was taking time off. Jared then decided to go to London for a few days to visit his girlfriend and their daughter.

Anything to buy time.

Time to pray for more time.

Sigh.

Logan walked outside to the wide balcony deck. The ship was still docked. He and his family —well, plus Marie—had boarded the ship first, ahead of all the rest of the passengers paying less for their staterooms.

He leaned against the plexiglass railings of his

balcony, at the edge of the ship—sun and wind in his hair—as he stared back into his stateroom. Marie had another stateroom just like this one. In between theirs, around the corner, Jonas and his nanny had a penthouse stateroom.

It was a splurge, but then Jonas was the birthday boy.

Still, Logan wondered what would become of his son if he continued to lavish such luxuries on a child who probably preferred the children's activity center and pool, and would only stay in his stateroom to sleep at night.

Then again, he was sure Jonas was going to be a good boy for all of them. He had always been such a good-natured boy. Calm and happy.

I wish Marie and I could be like that.

Logan felt bad all over again. He should apologize to her, but at the same time, he didn't want to.

Let her think what she will.

When Logan had chatted up that woman in the lunchroom, he had been fully aware that Marie was nearby. He wanted Marie to see that he had moved on.

Had he moved on, really?

When he had walked past her in a show of deliberate shunning...

He had felt terrible doing it.

He wanted to sit at her table and talk about Jonas, how much he had grown in the last three years she had been wasting her time in Europe.

Wasting?

Truth be told, Logan had no idea what Marie did in Europe these days. She hadn't been transparent about it ever since they had met more than six years ago. She had never come clean about the lies.

All he knew was that Marie Bouchard had not been a translator at all.

Beyond that, no amount of investigation could dig up who she was, except that she had been a translator. After a while, Logan stopped paying the private investigative firm.

As far as he was concerned, Marie Bouchard was not who she had said she was.

Was that even her real name?

It was as if Logan had married a mirage.

A chimera.

Still, she had mothered a child. There must have been some love there, yes?

Whether or not Marie confessed her dissimulations to God was of no concern to Logan. He knew that he himself had to be blameless before God.

For that reason, he had to apologize to Marie for being rude to her—the mother of his child.

He turned around to put both elbows on the wood railings. "Lord, why wouldn't Marie tell me the truth about who she really is and what she really does?"

The answer came to him quickly, just like that.

> *...for all have sinned and fall*
> *short of the glory*
> *of God.*

"Romans 3:23. Should've figured."

Logan hung his head, then warily emailed Marie.

~

*L*ogan dragged himself across the carpeted hallway between his stateroom and Marie's. He had emailed her, and she had ignored him.

Or he thought she had.

Logan wanted to get this gnaw off his chest so he could at least have a pleasant weekend before he dove into what would probably result in a big argument with his cousin on Monday over the failed investments they had made.

Until then, he wanted a quiet Saturday and Sunday, thank you very much.

Logan slowed down his steps, saying hello to the stewards greeting him, the entire time wondering what to say to Marie once he knocked on her door.

Six years prior, he had known what to say every time they were together, starting from their initial meeting at the French Riviera, and then ending in Atlanta.

Ending, indeed.

She had been beautiful, charming, sweet, and had spoken seven languages. After he had hired her for her first translation job for Urquhart Enterprises in Sweden, she then accompanied the Urquhart cousins to the various branch offices in Europe, translating for them in both business meetings and at social events. By the time they reached London, Logan was madly in love.

Madly?

Logan stopped outside Marie's door, and stood there.

Just stood there.

In some of their arguments throughout their short-lived marriage, Marie had accused him of having married her on the rebound. It could be true. Logan had been engaged to a twice-married wealthy businesswoman, who had abruptly broken off their engagement and had eloped with someone else to wherever.

Whatever.

Logan lifted his knuckles to knock on the heavy door. It opened before his hand reached it.

Marie peeked out through the partially open door.

"You're forgiven," she snapped.

And then she slammed the door in Logan's face.

CHAPTER FOUR

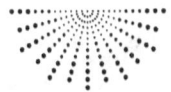

*S*ummoned by a child to a morning Bible study, Marie was only too eager to be there to have something to do while the cruise ship was at sea. Due to her jet lag, she had been up since three in the morning, and had gone to the gym and pool and back to her empty stateroom before sunrise.

However, now that she was sitting in the same space as her ex-husband, Marie didn't feel like she belonged, as if three years of being gone had erased all feelings of familiarity in this once-family.

The fifteen-minute Bible study had turned into twenty minutes, as little Jonas had insisted that Mrs. Ping read them the riot act—uh, participation rules—the first five minutes of the all-too-important meeting.

Everyone had to sit down quietly. No cell phones allowed. No texting.

"Sit and listen," Jonas had warned them twice.

"If you do not have a Bible, a paperback one will be provided for you," Mrs. Ping added. "We look at paper, not pixel."

Somewhere in the twenty-first minute, Marie thought she was going to snap.

"How did David cut off Goliath's head?" Jonas asked.

"What?" Marie gasped.

Sitting on the other side of Mrs. Ping, Logan must have seen Marie's concern. Instead of looking at his own Bible, he leaned over toward Mrs. Ping's large-print Bible, and started to mumble. "Ah, decapitation."

"I thought we're reading the children's Bible," Marie said. "He's only five."

"I'll be six next year, Mommy." Jonas tugged her arm.

Great.

Marie tried to even out her breathing. "Why don't we get to the details of decapitation later? Like when he's thirty years old."

"Decaf?" Jonas's eyes lit up. "Like coffee? Decaf coffee."

How did this child leap from decapitated to decaffeinated?

"Not decaf. I mean...uh, stuff like that. We'll talk about them when you're older, okay?"

"Stuff?" Jonas asked. "Did they stuff Goliath's—"

"Stop!" Marie pressed a hand to her chest.

"Mommy." Jonas shook his head. "I already know that David killed Goliath. I wanna know how he did it exactly. Did he use a light saber?"

Marie was about to respond when Logan raised his hand, as if to tell her he would handle it.

"Son, let's talk about onions," Logan said.

"Onions?" Jonas frowned, looking terribly confused. "Dad, David threw stones, not onions."

At this point, Marie felt a headache coming.

"Oh, look at the time." Logan tapped his Tag Heuer watch. "We're way past our fifteen-minute Bible study."

Jonas stared at his dad, the way Marie would stare at Logan at every quarrel, every fight, every disagreement in their marriage.

Logan broke the stare, turned to Mrs. Ping. Mouthed something.

To Marie, it looked like "help."

Mrs. Ping smiled calmly, as though she had been there, done that. "Since we're on Alaskan time, we can take a few more minutes to answer Mister Jonas's very good question."

The dark cloud over Jonas's face lifted. He looked like he was the most important person in the world.

"David obeyed God," Mrs. Ping said. "When we obey God, we don't always understand the details. They will be revealed to us by and by if God so allows."

Revealed to us by and by?

Marie wondered if Mrs. Ping was speaking above Jonas's head to her and Logan.

"God will tell us when we need to know." Mrs. Ping looked at Jonas.

Jonas seemed satisfied with the answer.

"That's what I was trying to get to," Logan said. "It's like peeling an onion. Layer by layer. We'll find out more and more."

"Well, that is, if you peel an onion all the way," Marie said. "I usually peel the skin, and chop up the rest—"

Marie's palm flew to her mouth.

Logan's eyes met hers. He seemed to know what she had meant. Yet, neither of them wanted to argue in front of Jonas, though they had done plenty of that when Jonas had been a baby.

Mrs. Ping had seen it all.

Marie pursed her lips.

We can't even agree on how to cut up an onion. How could we agree on marriage? On life?

"Children, let's not get distracted," Mrs. Ping broke the silence. "Jonas, what is the most important lesson we learn today from the story of David and Goliath?"

"Obey God no matter what," Jonas said. "Now can we go get ice cream?"

CHAPTER FIVE

*I*t had taken three adults to persuade little Jonas to postpone his cravings for ice cream until after lunch.

Does that mean I failed as a dad?

Logan wouldn't admit that in front of his ex-wife, but inside, he felt like his parenting skills were below par.

How many times had he let Jonas get his way, if only to keep the peace between father and son? Too many.

How many times had he prayed to God—his heavenly Father—for help? Too few.

Logan feared he was raising a manipulative brat, and what would he become when he grew up?

In the style of his now deceased Urquhart

grandfather, Jonas had cut a deal—yes, a deal!—to be compensated for his compliance. It hadn't seemed to be a difficult demand to meet when Jonas had first brought it up, but now...

Now, Logan was uncomfortable sitting next to Marie at their table in the formal dining room.

He didn't know why.

She smelled floral, with a hint of ocean. That French perfume suited her. Her hair was as wavy as ever, though she'd had it cut in such a way that its ends sat on her shoulders. With the Pacific sun shining on her hair, Logan could tell she hadn't colored it. It was the same chestnut hair she'd had since the first day they had met.

So why was he uncomfortable next to her?

He remembered the days when he couldn't wait to sit next to her, to wrap his hands around hers, to massage her neck, to whisper sweep nothings into her ear, as a loving husband would his bride.

All those were distant memories, rolling away like dry tumbleweeds across a dusty desert.

Across from them, Jonas sat next to Mrs. Ping.

Jonas stared at his parents. "Now I can see both of you together."

"You mean at the same time?" Logan corrected him.

"Sitting together at the same time."

Well, okay.

Marie hadn't said a word, and it was just as well. Every time she had opened her mouth, they had friction. Or perhaps, Logan had been reading too much into it. Perhaps he had been the friction.

Whatever. The point was that he and Marie were still not getting along.

The more he thought of it, the more he realized how different they both were. Logan didn't speak a lick of French, didn't care for French cuisine, didn't like the French Riviera. He was the meat-and-potato sort of guy, preferred greasy southern fried chicken anywhere in small town Georgia, and didn't care for seafood.

Like this lunch, for example. He had ordered lamb chops. She had poached halibut.

Why would anyone poach halibut? It's the grill for me.

If he were to ask Marie, she would probably say the reverse.

Why would anyone grill halibut?

Their differences went on and on. Marie wore what looked like a wool cardigan over her long-sleeved dress. She had always been cold. Back when they had been married, she would always shiver when Logan turned down the thermostat.

Always cold.

As for Logan, this room temperature could get cooler.

"I can't wait to see the whales," Logan declared as his hamburger and fries arrived.

Yep, taught my son well.

Meat and potatoes.

When everyone's lunch was served, it was time to ask God to bless the food. At that moment, Jonas said the unthinkable: "Let's hold hands."

To appease the little tyrant, Logan reached across the table to hold Jonas's right hand. The boy's left hand was in Mrs. Ping's hand. Her other hand was holding Marie's hand.

"Hold Mommy's hand," Jonas said.

Logan's hand was under the table. "How do you know we're not holding hands?"

"I know you, Dad," Jonas said.

Marie laughed. "Say please, love."

"Please hold Mommy's hand," Jonas asked again, politely but sternly.

Logan's jaw dropped at how quickly Jonas obeyed his mom.

And Logan did as he was told.

Marie's hand was smooth, like she had just applied lotion into it. Logan tried to recall the first time they had held hands way back when, but his recollections were interrupted by a loud *amen* from Jonas.

Uh oh.

He had missed the entire time they said grace. And God had seen it. Silently, he thanked God for the food and asked for forgiveness.

He felt a tug in his hand. He opened his eyes to find Marie trying to pull her hand away from his.

"Oh. Sorry." He was even sorrier to let go of her hand.

CHAPTER SIX

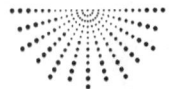

"*I* have to go to the little boys' room," Jonas declared halfway through his hamburger and chocolate milk.

Immediately, Logan put his napkin on the table. "I'll take him."

"You haven't finished eating." Mrs. Ping pointed to his plate. "I'll take him."

She doesn't get it.

Logan was trying to get away from Marie. If he didn't have to talk to her, there would be no confrontation. It was a preventive strategy that Urquhart men were known for.

Avoid all conflicts by fleeing the scene.

Mrs. Ping was on her feet and Jonas was already holding her hand, before Logan could come up with a reason to be the one to take Jonas to the boys' room.

Marie said not a word. She kept eating silently.

Logan placed the napkin back on his lap.

He glanced at her.

She didn't return the gesture.

Funny, she was even prettier than the day they had married. If he could do it all over again, he would give her a grand wedding. A destination wedding, even.

Sometimes Logan felt bad that, in spite of the Urquhart fortune, they'd had such a small beach wedding that only her parents and close relatives were invited to. Marie had insisted on not inviting too many people, and everyone was prohibited from posting the Urquhart-Bouchard wedding photos on social media.

After their mini honeymoon in Paris, Logan had to fly back to a string of meetings at the Urquhart Enterprise headquarters in Atlanta, and Marie had to go back to her translator job, wherever it was.

As crazy as it sounded, he would go out with her all over again, if only to revisit the times they had missed or lost. Perhaps he could court her, and let their relationship take its course from their being an item to being husband and wife.

They had leapt too quickly to the wedding altar, and then just as quickly, their marriage had fizzled out.

What on earth is a no-fault divorce anyway?

Had they admitted they'd made a mistake? How could anyone make a big mistake with such an important life event?

Well, I did.

Marie did.

Logan chewed into the last bit of lamb chops, juicy and cooked to his specifications. Still it would have tasted better had he been in a good mood.

There was no way now he could reboot his relationship with Marie. It was too late, wasn't it?

He glanced at her again. She was gazing out the windows. He could see a bit of her neckline. He remembered...

No. For all practical purposes, their relationship was over.

The only thing they had in common was parenthood. Even that, they could no longer do together.

"How's work?" Logan blurted.

That's original. Logan chided himself.

"Work?" Marie faced him. There was no frown on her face. It was cold. Like a steel in some wintry outdoors.

"I'm trying." That wasn't much of an explanation, but...

"To do what, exactly?" Marie asked. "To prevent us from killing each other the next five days?"

"We survived the first day."

"By avoiding each other."

"As long as you don't lop off my head like David did Goliath." Logan didn't know why he said that.

Marie laughed.

Oh I loved to hear that. Logan stared at her again.

"Parenting is hard, isn't it?" Marie asked. "So much harder than..."

Logan waited.

She didn't finish her sentence.

"Than what?" Logan asked.

"Than many things..." Marie seemed calm, but Logan could tell that something was percolating just beneath the surface.

"Like your job?"

Now Marie frowned a little. No one else would have been able to spot it, but Logan could. He could tell when she was upset at all, or starting to be.

"Why do you keep bringing up my job?" she

asked. "You said *work* earlier. How about asking me about my career?"

Logan felt a heartburn coming.

Should he say what was on his mind?

Here goes. "You chose it over us."

"Us?" Marie's eyes widened. "You and Jonas against me now?"

"Let's not fight."

Marie pushed back her chair.

"Where are you going?" Logan asked.

"None of your business." She picked up her purse from the floor on the other side of her chair.

"You can't leave," Logan said, almost in a panic.

"Why not?"

"Jonas will be back any minute now. He'll see you gone. Again."

All around them, the lunch crowd carried on. Nobody seemed to care that these two people were at it again. Everyone else seemed to be busy talking and eating. The servers in their white gloves circled the table. One came over to ask if they wanted their water goblets refilled.

Logan took the opportunity to reach out and touch Marie's arm.

To ask her to stay.

Don't go.

Please?

After the server left, Logan continued. "Whenever he asks for you, he's sad. Always sad."

Marie's lips moved slightly. Quavered?

"Don't make him sad. He just turned five last week. It has been three years without you in his young life."

"You blame me now?" Marie said between gritted teeth.

"I'm trying to avoid future psychological trauma in our son."

"Wait. What?" Marie pulled away from Logan's touch. She mumbled something in French.

Should have learned French. She could be cussing me out right now.

Logan waited.

"You're as much to blame for our broken family," Marie said.

"Who left? Who stayed?"

"I had no choice." Marie opened her mouth to say more. But for some reason, she decided not to.

"Choice? So you chose."

"If only you knew..."

"Knew what? Tell me."

"I can't." She pursed her lips.

"So there's another man?" Logan asked.

"No. There is no other. There hasn't been another."

"Me neither." The sudden realization that they both hadn't dated since their divorce hit Logan deep in his chest.

But.

There's this matter of transparency.

Maybe someday...

Logan motioned for her to sit down. "Please?"

Marie hesitated. Then she waved.

Logan looked in the direction of her wave, and saw Jonas bouncing back with Mrs. Ping in tow.

Marie sat down. "Only for ice cream."

"I'll take whatever I can get," Logan told her.

CHAPTER SEVEN

*I*t turned out there was more ice cream all afternoon on the top deck of the cruise ship—where the swimming pool was, with its noisy swimmers and splashers. At the rate Jonas was consuming all sorts of ice cream, Marie was sure he was going to be sick.

And forget nap time. All that sugar had to be used up first.

If Logan weren't busy with his work downstairs in his stateroom, he might have stopped Jonas from eating more ice cream than he already had. But Marie wasn't going to.

What's an extra scoop?

It wasn't like Jonas had this every week.

Sitting by the pool in tee shirt and shorts, Marie looked away from her son in the kiddie pool, playing with several other kids. Mrs. Ping was hovering over her charge, and Marie felt at ease enough to check her email.

The next time she looked up from her iPad, she spotted three men, two hijab-clad women, and one kid, heading her way, presumably toward the several empty teak lounge chairs around her. The kid pointed to the kiddie pool that Jonas was in, and he was escorted there by one of the women.

The men followed the second woman to the lounge chair nearby. Marie smiled, but the woman did not return it. She might not have noticed Marie there, with the sun shining down on them.

But the men.

Something about them made Marie curious. Having mingled with Arab immigrants in France, Marie felt that she knew more about the culture of the Middle Eastern region, but there was still a lot to learn.

To normal eyes, those three men looked like other vacationers from the Middle East, but to Marie, they looked like seasoned fighters. Were they armed?

Then again, she was probably paranoid. Still, in

her line of work, the best thing to do was not to appear too eager to learn, too inquisitive, too nosy.

The woman said nothing to the men. In fact, no one around Marie had spoken. She waited to see if she could spot the country they came from. But they had to speak first.

She didn't recall seeing them in the dining room. Perhaps they ate at the late seating. Or maybe they ate in the exclusive dining rooms or ordered room service.

She wondered which staterooms they were in. She didn't remember seeing them on her deck either.

In any case, the woman didn't seem to be prepared for a swim. She was covered from head to toe, but not in the modest swimming outfits that Marie had seem some conservative women wear. The other woman was dressed in a swimsuit that Marie had seen in the Middle East, but she did not go into the pool either.

Marie kept her eyes on her iPad, but her ears were listening.

Not a word.

She could hear the kids laughing and playing. She tried to pick up what they were saying so that she could determine a place of origin. The new kid were too cute for words. Marie guessed that he was about Jonas's age. The boy spoke in British English to Jonas and Mrs. Ping.

Marie waited for the men to speak, but they did not. Eventually the woman said something to the men about the weather being unexpectedly pleasant—

Arabic.

Marie strained to hear more.

No, no.

I'm on holiday. I'm not at work.

Besides, there were many languages on this cruise. Even though she could only speak seven languages, Marie could identity many other languages. She figured there were multiple languages spoken among the passengers, including English, Dutch—and Indonesian among the stewards.

Yes, listening ears were valuable in her work.

Work?

I'm not at work.

Logan had tried to remind her earlier that work had robbed her of her family time. Could that possibly be true?

Marie wondered if Logan had been really trying.

Ah, they would never be able to get along.

It's only for one week, Lord Jesus. Help me through this week.

Marie couldn't wait to fly home to...to...

Where was home?

Marseilles was her parents' home. Not hers.

In the last eighteen months she had been traveling everywhere. Home had been a suitcase and a bed, sometimes in a palace, but often in a dingy motel or a safe house.

Someday, she'd find a home. A real home.

When she swiped her iPad to get back to her emails, she saw that Logan had sent her a text message.

He wanted to know how Jonas was doing.

He's fine!

Marie didn't like his sort of inquiries at all. Was Logan questioning her motherhood? Chaining a guilt trip on her? She had been gone for almost half of Jonas's life, but she considered herself no different from a deployed soldier who had to leave her family behind for months at a time.

Logan should not hold that against me.

"Did you get my text?" Her ex-husband was standing at the end of her lounge chair. He was wearing a simple white shirt and a pair of crumpled canvas shorts.

"I didn't have time to respond," Marie said. "Can't you see we're busy here?"

"Sure you are. I can see you're doing more than nothing."

Marie pointed to the kiddie pool. "He's fine."

Mrs. Ping was talking to some other adults there. Jonas was laughing with the other kids. Then he rubbed his eyes.

"See that?" Logan tipped his sunglasses. "Past his nap time."

"I hate to take him away from his new friends."

"I'll do it then." Logan walked toward the kiddie pool.

Marie chuckled as Logan talked to Mrs. Ping instead of to Jonas directly.

Coward!

Logan walked back. "Told Mrs. Ping to give him five more minutes, and then he needs to shower and take a nap."

"Good."

"What's that smirk? You're laughing at me."

"I'm not." Marie kept a straight face.

"Are you questioning my parenting skills?"

"No comment."

Logan's jaw dropped. "Did you realize something?"

"What?"

"We're talking to each other."

Marie had to agree with him. "Because of Jonas."

"Our son."

Marie blinked. In the distance, Mrs. Ping was gathering Jonas's brightly colored towel and flip-flops.

"Take a walk with me?" Logan asked quietly. He looked like he expected Marie to say no.

She decided to surprise him. "I can't do it now, but how about after dinner tonight?"

"All right. It's a date then."

"Not a date," Marie countered. "We're trying to get along so we don't ruin our son's life."

"Okay, a business meeting then."

"If you put it that way." Marie put down her iPad. "Maybe we can discuss what excursions we want to do the rest of the week."

Five days seemed like an eternity now that she thought about it.

"That's easy. Whatever Jonas wants to do, we do," Logan said.

"Ah, child-directed parenting."

"Is that the name for it?"

Jonas and Mrs. Ping walked toward them. Jonas looked awfully tired.

"I guess the ice cream has worn off," Marie said.

"Either that, or it's the after-sugar effect." Logan laughed.

"What's that?"

Logan shrugged. "Don't know. I'm just making up hyphenated words, like you did."

"That's supposed to help our non-relation-ship?" Marie snapped.

Oh, why did I do that?

"Ah, irritable. Maybe you need a nap too," Logan said.

"Mommy." Jonas tugged at Marie's arm. "Will you stay with me in my room?"

"Sure." Marie talked to Mrs. Ping. "Take the afternoon off. Go to the spa. Get your hair done. Or something. Have fun."

"Good idea," Logan added. "Don't worry about the bill. Tell them I'll take care of it."

"Wow. Thank you." Mrs. Ping's eyes bright-ened. "I'll get him showered and dressed for nap time, and then I'll go."

Marie wasn't sure if Mrs. Ping realized that she wouldn't know what to do with Jonas at nap time, but she was glad not to have to ask for help with getting Jonas ready. Doing so in front of Logan would only make him think the worst of her.

How could any birth mother give up her only child?

Marie had her reasons.

Certainly, God had sent Mrs. Ping to fill in where Marie had been unable to fulfill her job.

Oh how she longed to be Jonas's mother again.

Truly be. Not from a distance, but there, right there with her own son.

Something I need to pray about.

CHAPTER EIGHT

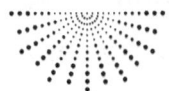

$\mathcal{W}$alking in the moonlight on one of the decks of the cruise ship sailing across the waters could have been romantic, but not for this pair with their irreconcilable differences.

Which, Logan was certain, had been primarily due to their geography and career choices. They had clearly failed in their long-distance marriage. Marie wouldn't leave her job in Europe, and Logan couldn't leave his job in Atlanta, Georgia.

Other than that, they had produced a gorgeous child—when he wasn't trying to manipulate his parents into giving him everything he wanted.

Case in point: this birthday cruise.

"If we keep giving him what he wants, we'll run

out of ability or means to do so before he's twenty-one," Marie said.

She was dressed modestly in a dark purple dress. Cruise dinners used to be rather formal affairs, but today's cruises no longer required its patrons to dress up in tuxedos and gowns before they entered the main dining room. While the dress code wasn't golf casual, no one needed to show up looking like they were attending a wedding or a funeral.

Logan liked Marie's simple dress. She had on strapped heels, but the dress was long-sleeved.

He wondered now if she was cold. She hadn't brought her cardigan.

"Right?" Marie waited.

"I hear you, but we'll cross that bridge when we get there." It was the best answer Logan could think of at this point. He wished that—

He didn't know what he could wish for. He wanted to be the best dad ever for Jonas, but he had so much work to do at the office that he had left the parenting to Mrs. Ping most of the time.

Although Marie had been an absentee mother, Logan hadn't done much better, even though he was in town and lived in the same house as his own son.

One could be in the same house and be distant,

be strangers, be out of touch with the rest of the family.

Lord, I don't know how to be Jonas's dad.

"You're going to get there sooner than you think," Marie said.

Logan stopped walking. They were standing across the deck from more lounge chairs. On the other side of the railings were lifeboats.

"Me?" Logan asked. "I thought you said *we* earlier."

"We're not together in this. I'll go back to Paris soon, and you'll have to raise Jonas on your own. You have full custody. Remember that expensive court battle I could not afford?"

"I'm not sure if I want to do this alone anymore," Logan said. "I'm thinking I need to start dating."

"You don't need my permission."

Marie's French accent slipped out. It was then that Logan knew she was bothered by his declaration.

How could she be?

We're divorced.

"It gets complicated when we marry other people." Logan waited for Marie to respond.

Yes, he wanted to know what was on her mind.

They began walking again.

"Life itself is complicated." Marie shrugged, as if she had on a mask. "When you have a blended family, it adds to the complexity."

"I'm trying to simplify my life, but I hate being alone."

"Me too." Marie's eyes widened even as she said it, as if it had been a mistake.

Another slip of the tongue?

"You too?"

"I take that back." She stiffened. "My life is so busy. I don't have time..."

"I hate to wake up one day when I'm seventy, and find out I missed out on life and love," Logan said.

Marie leaned against the railing.

Logan joined her.

A number of decks below, the Pacific Ocean swooshed against the hull of the massive cruise ship. Sparkles of moonlight glittered on the deep, deep ocean.

The horizon was dark, morphed into the steel-gray night. In the sky, the moon shone down. There were some stars sparkling in the distance.

Moon and stars and the sky that God had made. Signs that life went on.

Life went on in spite of Marie and me.

Logan breathed in deeply. There was nothing

he wanted to ask of her. Not anymore. Their life, as they had known it, was over. Now they had to do whatever they could to make things work out for Jonas, so that he too could grow up, out of these ashes, into a beautiful and productive life.

"We need God's help. His mercy. His grace," Logan said.

"Yes. His everything."

"You know what's funny?" Logan chuckled. "Marriage and parenting are harder than getting an MBA, and running a business."

"Or chasing..." Marie paused.

"Chasing? Chasing what?"

Marie didn't say. Instead, she said something else. "Apart from Christ, we fail."

Logan knew that verse by heart. His mom had made him memorize it as a child. "John 15:5. 'I am the vine, you are the branches. He who abides in Me, and I in him, bears much fruit; for without Me you can do nothing.' That verse?"

Marie nodded.

Logan left his earlier question unanswered. When she wanted to talk, she could talk. No point pressuring her to be transparent with him. They were no longer married.

The more important thing right now was for their family—their son, primarily—to be in God's perfect will. Logan's pastor at Midtown Chapel back in Atlanta had said that God could restitch all these torn sections of the tapestry.

Logan feared it might be too late for Jonas. They had already ruined his young life. Still, he felt that he and Marie had made some progress—what little progress this might be. "Would you..."

Marie looked at him.

"Would you walk with me again before this cruise is over?" Logan asked.

Ask not, get not.

"Why not? We're pretty much stuck together until Saturday," Marie said.

"After dinner tomorrow night?"

"An excuse to stuff ourselves with Baked Alaska and so forth?"

"It's the meringue," Logan explained. "Light and fluffy it might be, but it has devastating effects."

Marie grinned. "That's one thing I like about you."

"Just one thing?"

"Don't push it."

"And what might be that one thing, pray tell?"

"You make life sound easy," Marie said. "My job is difficult and dangerous. You provide the counterpunch."

Dangerous? "What's dangerous about being a translator? I can't imagine..."

"Any job can be dangerous, metaphorically speaking."

She had backtracked.

"Uh-huh." Logan didn't like what he heard, but he wasn't about to spoil the night. He didn't know why he had asked her to walk with him again.

And she had said yes.

Let's not ruin future moments.

Marie said nothing else, and neither did Logan ask her any more questions, as they spent the next moments looking out to sea in silence.

CHAPTER NINE

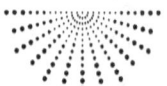

*M*arie held one of Jonas's hands, and Logan held the other, making their son as happy as a bee, as they walked from the tour bus to the picnic area outside Juneau, where the aroma of smoked and grilled salmon mingled in the air, weaving in and out of the large crowd waiting for the lunch this Monday.

Marie almost talked over Jonas's head, but she'd have to shout to be heard. Besides, she didn't want to be the first to talk to Logan. So far, he had initiated conversations with her.

Whatever had happened between them still simmered below the surface. They could have tension at any time. Why instigate that?

Logan was on the phone now, and Marie could

clearly hear the conversation. If she could advise him, she'd tell him not to discuss multi-million-dollar acquisitions on an unsecured cell phone in a tourist spot with at least a thousand people waiting for their baked wild Alaskan salmon.

Then again, Logan hadn't asked for her opinion.

He had never once asked for her thoughts on anything other than where to eat out on the Friday evenings he let his personal chef take the night off.

Perhaps in his mind, Marie was nothing more than a translator. A businesswoman she might not be, but she sure knew how to be discreet, right?

There was so much Marie wanted to tell Logan about what she really did in real life. But he wouldn't believe her nor understand. Perhaps he wouldn't even care. After all, he hadn't bothered to find out the truth. Or he hadn't tried hard enough.

That private investigator that Logan had sent... There was no way he'd find out anything beneath the surface.

She had told him the truth about her name, her hometown, and her day job. Yes, she had earned a master's degree in linguistics. Yes, she was a certified translator. However, she also had other training.

Other...things.

"Right, Mom?" Little Jonas tugged at her blouse.

It reminded her of when he had been a baby, clinging to her shoulders and chest as she carried him everywhere on her hip.

She missed those days of motherhood.

How many more years of Jonas's life would she miss?

Would Jonas grow up remembering happy moments with her at all, or would he always think of her as the mother who had left him.

My boy is growing up faster than I can keep up with his life.

Soon, she'd head back to France, to her undercover work, and this dream family vacation would simply be a memory marker, a vapor once again.

"What is it, love?" Marie asked gently, not wishing for her moment with Jonas to end. Maybe if she could remember this time, she wouldn't feel too bad later.

"I can eat a whole fish!" Jonas said. It seemed to be a repeat of something Marie had missed hearing. "Right, Mom?"

"Depends on the size of the fish. Some fish are so huge that they could feed many people."

"Wow. Can God make such a big fish?"

"God made all fish, love," Marie said. "He is the Creator of all. He also created you and me."

"And Daddy too," Jonas added.

Marie nodded. "And Daddy too."

Logan pocketed his iPhone. "And Daddy what?"

Marie didn't answer.

"God gave me Mommy and Daddy," Jonas said.

Logan grunted as his iPhone pinged again. He was back on it, swiping, tapping, disappearing into his business zone. Pretty soon, he let go of Jonas's hand.

The look on Jonas's face pulled at Marie's heart.

In the distance, another tour bus disgorged more people. If they didn't hurry, there would be no place for the Urquhart family to sit anymore.

They had to find three empty seats at any table before lunch was served. One parent had to stay with Jonas while the other parent went to get drinks and plasticware. Mrs. Ping wasn't with them because she had opted to check out the Mendenhall Glacier instead. And Logan wasn't helping.

Marie felt like she had to...

And she did.

She stepped in front of Logan and peeled that

phone off his ear. She turned it off, and slid it into her own purse. "Your son is more important."

Logan looked stunned.

Positively stunned.

CHAPTER TEN

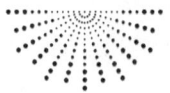

When they rode the tour bus to go to their other excursion today, Logan was reconciled with his phone. Suddenly, his brain could function again.

Lunch hadn't taken very long, but he was glad that Marie had hinted at his helpfulness. All he had done was secure three seats at a table and carried lemonade for everybody. Hardly anything earth-shattering like the new business deal he was trying to sort out.

Once again, his cousin Jared had done it. While in London visiting his girlfriend and their child, Jared had played golf with one Colm Cargill, who had known him through mutual friends in Savannah, Georgia. It had turned out that Cargill

Internet Communications would like to open a new branch in the United States, and was looking for investors.

Now Jared wanted Urquhart Enterprises to drop the steel merger in favor of software.

Earlier, at the salmon bake, Logan had been in the middle of texting his thoughts to Jared, when Marie yanked his phone out of his hands. Now that he had gotten it back, Logan realized that it was almost seven o'clock in London, and Jared was at dinner with his girlfriend.

Across the bus aisle, Marie and Jonas sat together. It was way past Jonas's nap time, but they weren't going back to the cruise ship docked at the port of Juneau until later this afternoon. So there he was, his head on Marie's lap, taking a power nap. His knees bent, shoes pushed against the wall of the bus at the window sill.

Logan was glad that Jonas had decided to sit with his mom instead of with him. He had to catch up on all the emails he had missed the last ninety minutes they had been at the salmon bake.

There was so much to do.

His corporate attorney was waiting for his reply. He wanted to send an email to his cousin. He had to find out more about the Cargills. Of course, Logan's cousin would have his Ruttledge Yamada

Urquhart Commercial Properties build the new Cargill-Urquhart software buildings in the USA.

Logan made a mental note to call his cousin to see if there had been any prospective land in metro Atlanta. Or Fulton County. Or Hall County where the property taxes were low—

The screen blacked out.

"No, no, no!" He should have recharged the battery overnight. He knew it has been red for a while, but he was confident he wouldn't run out of juice.

He let out a growl.

Someone tapped his shoulder. There was Marie's outstretched hand, offering him a battery pack.

"Lifesaver." Logan plugged it into his phone. "Thanks."

Marie simply nodded. On her lap, Jonas was sleeping, his long legs looking for a place to stretch. That boy would probably grow up to be as tall a Logan—or taller.

"What else do you carry in that purse?" Logan asked.

She smiled but said nothing.

CHAPTER ELEVEN

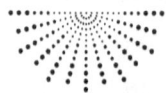

hen the tour bus stopped at the dock, Jonas bounced right out of his seat after his power nap. Now he wanted his daddy to carry him. Marie didn't like to hear him whine.

"Whose bright idea was it to go from a salmon bake to whale watching?" Logan frowned.

"Yours, brilliant one," Marie said.

"I'm going to be so wiped out by the time we get back to the ship. Not sure if I can eat dinner."

Marie said nothing. She and Logan were different there. When Logan was tired, he chatted non-stop. When she was tired, she didn't speak.

Which also meant she wasn't in the mood for a conversation.

In fact, at this moment, her eyes looked longingly away into the distance, toward the row of cruise ships at the nearby port. She could skip the whale watching trip, get a taxi cab or Uber ride back to their ship, go to her stateroom, and take a nap.

This jet lag was making her groggy at all the wrong times of the day.

Still, they exited the bus, looking like a proper family.

Logan carried Jonas on his shoulders, and led the way down the steps of the dock to the double-decker catamaran. The boat was crowded, mostly with cruise ship passengers.

Marie recognized a few faces from their ship's dining room, poolside, and children's play area.

"Mommy!" Still clinging to his dad's head, Jonas pointed. "My new friend Abdul. See him?"

Well, Marie might be a few inches shorter than Logan, but Jonas's head cleared both of theirs. She faced the direction where Jonas had pointed, but saw no hijab, no entourage, no Abdul. Still, she nodded, giving her son the benefit of doubt.

After a snack of smoked wild Alaskan salmon on crackers—delicious!—they made their way to the top deck to find somewhere to sit. Jonas was too excited for words, and Marie was only too happy to let Logan deal with him. It was past Jonas's nap time, and that second wind was wearing down Marie.

It didn't even faze Logan. He was calm and collected, and let Jonas bounce all over him.

Oddly enough, he hadn't used his phone once on the trip out on the catamaran, and neither had he returned the phone charger to her.

With Jonas between them making noise, there had been no opportunity for Marie and Logan to talk.

Just as well.

Some things could never be the same again.

All they had between them was Jonas.

Someday, Jonas would be eighteen, go to college, and then that was the end of it.

Marie closed her eyes, and nearly fell asleep, except for the fidgety Jonas next to her. He was yakking away about whales and whatever.

Over the intercom, the announcement came about their arrival somewhere.

For some reason, Marie didn't feel like leaving her seat. "I'll stay right here and take a nap."

Jonas looked like he was about to cry.

"What?" Marie wrinkled her eyebrow. Clearly she had missed all the *instructions* Jonas had been trying to give her.

"You're coming with us. Now, Mommy."

The crowd around them moved outside.

"I want to be in front," Jonas said.

Marie sighed. She didn't want to spoil the party.

She was surprised when Logan reached out and pulled her to her feet, like an invitation to a dance...

CHAPTER TWELVE

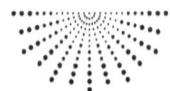

*T*he humpback whale calls were difficult to imitate, but Logan and Jonas made a go at it and tried their best as they watched the whales breach the water surface and then splash back into their comfort zone.

In unison, father and son made a mess of the whale song. Logan knew they were laughable, but it had made Jonas happy that Dad had sung along.

"You two sound like some pathetic frogs trapped in a sewer," Marie said, almost nonchalantly.

Logan glanced at Jonas.

"I'm a whale, not a frog!" Jonas spread his arms wide.

Now he looked like a stampeding elephant in

the crowd of tourists on the catamaran, but Logan wasn't about to say anything. He waited for Marie to do the honors.

This time, Marie didn't say a word.

Jonas tried his whale song again, alone. Somewhere in the crowd someone laughed. It was probably about something else, but somehow it affected Jonas. His face sagged. He began to cry.

Logan swept him up into his arms and pointed toward the swimming whales, now squirting water into the air. "Look at that, Jonas!"

He had no idea what Marie was doing behind them now, but he didn't care. This trip, this cruise, was primarily for Jonas. It was part of his boy's birthday present, and Logan was determined to make it count.

Their cruise had barely started—well, it was the third day—and the last thing Logan wanted was a pouty kid to take home this weekend.

Why can't Marie just play along?

A hand touched his arm. He didn't have to look. He knew who that hand belonged to.

I so miss her touch.

But it was over between them.

The hand remained on his arm.

He didn't hear her say anything, but he knew she was sorry about what she had blurted without thinking. He wanted to tell her it was okay, but it wouldn't be true.

It wasn't okay. Their son was only five years old, and took things literally. Logan felt sorry that Marie hadn't had the privilege of being mommy to Jonas.

Whose fault is that?

Certainly not his. He had done all he could to save the marriage. Marie had wanted out long before they had met the marriage counselor at church.

She had checked out of their marriage as soon as her maternity leave was over, always gone on assignments in Europe. Logan couldn't imagine what was so important that she couldn't take time off to be with her son or her husband.

If Logan had known that she would be in absentia, he wouldn't have married her at all.

Then again...

Here they were, like a family again.

Jonas in his arms.

His wife by his side—

Ex-wife.

Logan watched Marie—oblivious to his thoughts—pull out her phone and take photos.

No, she was filming a video.

He followed her gaze.

She was pointing at the whales, the sea, the sky, and then at the people all around them, then to the mountain ranges in the distance, and then back to the people and crowd.

Back and forth.

Logan wondered what on earth she was up to, panning across the crowd, but he didn't want to spoil the moment—whatever moment it seemed to be.

On the ride back to shore, they listened to a lecture on whale baleen. Logan thought that Jonas might be excited to see how big and long a baleen really was, but the boy was fast asleep.

And so was Marie.

Her head rested right on his other shoulder. Just like she used to do a long time ago when they had traveled together on trains across Europe. In between her assignments as a translator and his business meetings, they had taken excursions with some friends.

Logan remembered their favorite spot in Budapest, the city where they had their first kiss. It had seemed like ages ago, though it had only been six or seven years.

The memory surprised him.

Maybe, just maybe, there was still something left between him and Marie...

Nah.

They had parted ways under a cloud of distrust and mistrust. Unresolved problems did not a happy relationship make.

Still, Marie had been a good sport all day—for the most part.

He remembered her faraway stares on the tour bus earlier this afternoon, like she had longed for something missing.

Truth be told, he did too.

He had their son to raise. But more than him, Logan wanted his wife back.

But how, Lord Jesus? How?

Marie's head shifted on his shoulder, and now her hands wrapped around his arm. He didn't move at all, in case she stirred and left his side.

Lord, our marriage broke and shattered. Can You put it together again?

Immediately, Logan answered his own question.

Sure, You can, Lord.

But would it be best for us?

CHAPTER THIRTEEN

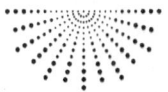

*B*ack onboard the cruise ship, they had almost ordered room service, but Jonas woke up from his second power nap of the day to declare that he wanted to eat dinner with his new friend, Abdul.

Mrs. Ping tried to get him to sleep until four o'clock—only fifteen minutes away—but it was a fruitless exercise in frustration.

Marie felt sorry for Jonas because he was an only child. Accompanied by three adults—Dad, Mom, and a nanny—Jonas didn't have his regular friends from kindergarten back in Atlanta with him.

After listening to Jonas whine for two minutes,

Marie gave in. "Dinner isn't until six o'clock. Maybe he could play with his friends for a little bit, if we can coordinate the time. Do you happen to know how to contact them?"

Mrs. Ping didn't know, but Jonas did.

"Abdul said he's going to be in the playroom when they get back," Jonas said in some weird kid's voice that didn't sound natural. It was whiny, and grated on Marie.

"Who taught him to whine?" Marie blurted to Mrs. Ping.

"I don't know, ma'am." Suddenly formal, Mrs. Ping busied herself with putting away Jonas's sneakers in their small closet.

Who else but Logan? Spoiling our son.

"Jonas, say that again in a normal tone," Marie said. "I don't speak whiny language."

Jonas's lips quivered.

Mrs. Ping interjected and offered to take Jonas to the playroom to meet his friend, Abdul.

"No, Mrs. Ping. I will take him myself—but only after he stops whining."

Everyone was silent.

"Mommy," Jonas said in a normal voice.

"Yes, son?"

"May we go to the playroom?"

"Of course." Marie reached for his hand.

Jonas jumped up and down.

"Go to the spa or something," Marie told Mrs. Ping. "We'll see you at dinner."

"But I'm paid to do this."

Even as the nanny protested, Marie could tell that she would welcome extra time off.

"Don't worry. When I go home to France, you'll have your hands full twenty-four seven. Enjoy your rare days off, yes?"

Nodding, Mrs. Ping started tidying up the stateroom.

"They have stewards for that," Marie told her.

"I know."

"Don't clean the bathrooms while you're trying to get something done. Go to the spa. I'll pay for it."

"Thank you, ma'am."

"Marie."

And then mother and son skipped happily out of the stateroom, toward the elevator.

Holding hands with an exuberant and chatty child was something Marie had missed for several years. The last time she had spent any time alone with her son, he had been in diapers.

Chatty, he had not been.

She wondered if Jonas had taken after Logan more.

As for Marie, she had always been the quiet,

observant one. Preferring to listen rather than talk, her own personality had served her well in her profession.

The one Logan doesn't know about.

CHAPTER FOURTEEN

*S*itting at the Lego table with Jonas, across from the hijab-wearing woman—who had introduced herself through her assistant as simply Aliyah with no last name—Marie was certain that the Middle Eastern mother had more to say to her, but either her English was not so good or she wasn't allowed to talk to strangers.

"Do you speak French?" Marie asked, trying to build some sort of bridge.

Aliyah shook her head.

That told Marie that Aliyah understood her question in English.

She glanced at the assistant sitting next to Aliyah. It was the same woman who had accompanied her and the two kids. Their facial features were alike, and Marie had almost mistaken them to be related.

Aliyah had called the woman her *assistant*, but left it at that. Marie wanted to ask what kind of assistant she was, but she did not want to raise any suspicion about her own curiosity.

For all she knew, there was nothing going on beneath the surface, although in Marie's mind, Aliyah's assistant behaved more like a handler who had censored Aliyah's words and phrases when she translated on the fly from Arabic to English. Perhaps to protect her? Or was it something else?

It was a not a good thing for the two ladies that Marie could understand Arabic.

Aliyah's two boys and Jonas decided to leave the Lego table to build a megastructure on a giant round rug mere feet away from them, where several other kids were playing. They didn't have the same language barriers as the adults. They spoke Lego, and they spoke playtime.

Marie could now cast her vote for their country of residency. It could be the United Kingdom, but it could also be any of the European countries, whose citizens spoke English more British than American. One thing she was quite sure of: the boy did not speak Australian English.

"I left my camera in my room. Could you get it

for me?" Aliyah asked her assistant in Arabic. "I want to take photos of Abdul to send to his father."

"I cannot leave you, your highness."

Your highness?

Marie's face was still turned toward the three boys at play. She smiled and clapped along when Jonas cheered, like she wasn't paying attention to the two women at her table.

"If you give me back my phone, I will call Zaid to get my camera," Aliyah suggested.

If you give me back my phone...

Marie pretended she didn't understand their conversation in Arabic. She didn't even look at Aliyah, but she could sense that the princess's voice was somewhat under duress.

It struck Marie as strange. Why was Aliyah not allowed her own phone?

Is she a prisoner? Surely not on a cruise ship.

The translator called the man named Zaid. "I don't know where it is. Look for it. I cannot leave here, and Abdul is still playing."

A few minutes later, one of the three guards, whom Marie had seen at the poolside the day before, walked into the playroom. He was carrying a GoPro camera. He glanced at Marie, then at Aliyah and her aide.

Marie tried to commit his name and face to memory. Zaid.

She wondered what sort of photos were in the GoPro camera—

Stop!

I'm on holiday—vacation—whatever!

"Mommy, look!" Jonas waved what looked like a clump of Lego blocks stuck together. "Guess what this is?"

Oh, no. Don't make me guess, son. "Uh...a ball?"

"Noooo..." Jonas looked hurt, as though his mom had to guess it right at first try.

"I'll take a picture of it." Marie walked toward Jonas, snapping away with her iPhone.

"Is it a boat?" She walked around Jonas, taking more photos—with Aliyah and her escorts around her at the table.

"Nooo, Mommy. Guess again." Jonas made a whooshing sound.

"A plane?" Snap. Snap.

Jonas made a face at his poor mom. "A helicopter!"

Marie laughed. "I would never have guessed."

Snap. Snap.

She pocketed her phone as soon as the man— Zaid, right—started walking toward her. She quickly knelt down by Jonas. "Want me to build a plane?"

Jonas nodded his head vigorously. "Then we can have an air battle!"

Marie sat right in the middle of the group of kids, picked up a few Lego blocks and tried to make the best of it. From the corner of her eye, she noticed Zaid backing off.

Aliyah was saying something to him, but Marie couldn't hear her, on account of the noisy kids.

When she showed her Lego pieces to her son, Marie stole a look past his ears.

The assistant motioned for Zaid to leave the room.

Ah, so we know who's in charge, calling the shots.

It certain fit the narrative in Marie's mind that the assistant is Aliyah's handler. She could also be her personal protector, technically speaking. But it begged the question why. Why were they in Alaska, on this particular cruise?

Pretty soon, a couple of children younger than Jonas had joined the big play rug. For some reason, one of the little girls sat down on Marie's lap.

"That's my mommy," Jonas declared.

Nice to be acknowledged.

When Marie looked up to ask Aliyah to join them, she was gone. Did she leave with Zaid?

The assistant came over, calling for the two boys, telling them it was time to leave.

The boys fussed, but she said they had to get ready for dinner. Their meal with special dietary needs would be ready for them soon, and their mother wouldn't want their food to be cold.

It all sounded normal.

Marie smiled and waved goodbye to the assistant, but was ignored.

Well, you have a nice evening too.

CHAPTER FIFTEEN

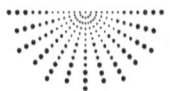

"Something on your mind?" Logan asked Marie at dinner.

She hadn't spoken a word since they sat down, and had barely mumbled *amen* when they said grace before eating.

Marie didn't answer. Maybe she didn't hear him. Logan decided not to press. Something was clearly on her mind.

Across the table from them, Jonas was eating chicken fingers.

Ten thousand dollars for this trip, and all the kid ordered were chicken fingers.

"We came all the way to Alaska for fast food," Logan said.

He glanced at Marie. She was smiling.

That's my girl.

Logan wished he could be her confidant. He wished she would talk to him and tell him everything about herself, her life, her career.

Three years of marriage had not been enough time for them to know each other, with Marie gone ninety percent of the time.

Maybe this cruise ship was a second chance from God for them to reconnect, reinforce the tenuous thread that had been their marital relationship.

For Jonas's sake, Logan would at least try. The poor kid had spent the last three years without his mother. A phone call here and there did not a bond make.

Logan had almost remarried for Jonas to have a live-in mother, but Lexi Parker wasn't the one for him, contrary to what everyone else had thought. Lexi only wanted to live in his twenty-room estate and drive his car collection.

On the other hand, Marie didn't want a thing from him. Not a dime.

In Logan's heart, he knew he could only love her. However, she was so far away, so distant from him that he wondered if he had been in love with only a mirage.

"Marie?" Logan tried to get her to talk.

She lifted her head.

"Are we walking tonight?"

She halfway nodded.

It seemed like a partial commitment, but Logan was going to hold her to it.

Mrs. Ping had said nothing throughout much of the dinner, only paying attention to wiping specks of food off Jonas's face.

One thing caught Logan's attention. Mrs. Ping grinned a lot this evening. If he didn't know any better...

"Have you met someone?" Logan asked her. Maybe? How would anyone know such things?

At first, Mrs. Ping looked stunned. Then she smiled again, like a giddy schoolgirl, peeling back forty years of her life.

"That's wild," Marie said.

Her first two words after the whispered *amen.*

We're making progress.

Mrs. Ping's face reddened.

"Let's not put her on the spot." Marie's hand was on Logan's arm—like she had often done when she wanted his attention at those parties they would attend in Europe, meeting diplomats, heads of state, rich businessmen and businesswomen.

Logan glanced at her. He had no idea what was in her mind. He dared not guess.

"Are we having fun so far, Jonas?" Logan asked.

He felt Marie retract her hand from his arm.

Maybe I shouldn't have changed the subject.

"I want to see the whales again." Jonas pouted.

"We saw many whales today, didn't we?" Logan asked.

Jonas nodded. "I want to buy a whale."

"God owns the whales. They belong in the ocean." Logan realized that they hadn't bought any whale souvenirs. "When we get to the next town, we can get you a whale cushion or something."

"I don't want a cushion, Daddy."

"A stuffed plushie, then?"

"Okay. Where are we going?" Jonas dipped his chicken in the little ketchup bowl.

"I think we stop at Skagway first, then Ketchikan."

"Catchy? Do they have geezers there?"

Mrs. Ping looked stunned. Marie nearly choked on her water.

"We'll see the glaciers when we sail through the Inside Passage," Logan explained.

"What are we going to do in Catchy?"

"Ketchikan. What do you want to do? Go on a

boat? Walk in the forest? See the salmon hatch-ery?" Logan asked.

"That sounds fun," Mrs. Ping said.

Logan waited, but Marie said nothing.

That made him wonder why.

CHAPTER SIXTEEN

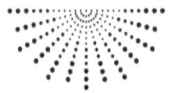

Marie was glad for the cloud cover tonight. Otherwise, with the moon out, Logan might recall their moonlight walks just like in the days. She didn't want him to have any idea that they were getting back together again. The last time she checked, Logan wouldn't leave the United States, and she couldn't leave Europe.

"What went wrong with us?" Logan asked. His voice was as gentle as the breeze that floated across the top deck of the ocean liner.

Around them, groups of people gathered here and there, some chatting and laughing away. Some walking, some on deck chairs, some attempting to read with clip-on nightlights. The deck below them was filled with people, both in the pool and poolside.

Somewhere behind Logan and Marie, glass doors led to the piano lounge. Every now and then, when someone opened those doors, Marie could hear a jazzy number.

She drew a deep breath of the Alaskan air. It was a cool June evening. She had buttoned up her cardigan before they left the dining room.

If not for the company, it would have been just another evening out at sea.

What went wrong with us?

Logan's question hung in the air.

"I can't remember," Marie finally said.

"Neither can I." Logan seemed to have prepared his answer since it came so quickly after hers.

"Maybe we were too young to be married," Marie suggested.

"I was thirty-one, and you were twenty-nine. I think we knew what we were doing."

"Maybe."

"On the other hand, you might be right," Logan added. "If fifty is the new forty, and forty is the new thirty..."

"Then we were acting like teens?" Marie asked.

Logan sighed. "We fought over what we knew not of, when we should have surrendered a lot of things into God's hands. He knows all things, whereas our own understanding is finite."

"Jeremiah 33:3 says, 'Call to Me, and I will answer you, and show you great and mighty things, which you do not know.' We should have called out to God. He would have shown us what to do."

Logan nodded. He stopped by a railing.

Marie stopped too, if only to look fourteen decks down to the ocean. The waves were dark and looked mysterious in the cloudy night, but God held up the ship, didn't He?

How could He not have held up our marriage?

"Tell me the truth, Marie. If you had more time to think about our whirlwind romance, would you have gone out with me six years ago?"

Marie shrugged.

"You're not sure," Logan said quietly.

"I'm never sure when I'm with you, Logan." Her eyes were somewhere else.

Coming out of the piano lounge, two men started to light up near the *No Smoking* zone. They were two of the three bodyguards that accompanied Aliyah, her son, and her assistant, everywhere they went onboard the ship.

One of them spoke on his cell phone. Marie could not read his lips from this far away.

"Let's keep walking," she suggested to Logan.

"Whatever you want." Logan followed Marie.

She led them close to the men. In the moonless night, Marie and Logan were well hidden in the shadows. She held Logan's hand at one point, and it seemed to have caught him by surprise. She tried to prevent them from directly facing the two men by stopping at the railing every now and then. For all practical purposes, they did look like a couple on an evening stroll.

Downwind now, she could hear faint Arabic. One of the languages that Marie spoke, it had been the second non-French language she had picked up, after English. There were Arabic communities in Paris during some of her childhood years not spent in Marseilles, offering her many opportunities to practice speaking almost daily.

"Take them?" The man with the phone nodded. "I'll wait for your call."

Take them?

Them who?

Take them when? Where?

Marie checked herself. Maybe she was mistaken. For all she knew, the man could mean take Aliyah and her son on the next excursion. They would arrive in Skagway by morning, and had all day to roam the area.

However, if the INTERPOL information had been any indication, it was more than a vacation for Aliyah and her son. The data were sketchy, and she had been told to remain on standby for further instructions, if any were required.

The men were coming toward them. Marie leaned against Logan. He wrapped his arm around her. She didn't push him away. She couldn't.

"What's going on?" Logan whispered in her ear and wrapped an arm around her waist.

Marie heard footsteps behind them.

"Infidels!" One of the men snarled in a low voice.

Logan must have heard it. Marie could feel his arm stiffen as tried to pull it away so he could turn around. She felt as though he was about to respond to the remark.

She ran her hand up his arm, as smoothly as possible, as if she herself didn't hear the insult. She cupped Logan's face with her hands, pulling his forehead toward hers, obscuring their faces from the men coming toward them.

Marie had no idea what message she was

sending to Logan, but he took over, caressing his lips over her cheek and chin and then...

Their lips met.

For a long moment, Marie forgot everything else.

CHAPTER SEVENTEEN

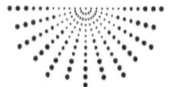

*a*fter breakfast, Logan and Marie—with Jonas in between them—marched down the gangway connecting the cruise ship to Skagway. It was barely eight o'clock, but there were already many ship passengers walking about.

Logan wanted to ask Marie what happened between them on the top deck the night before, but he wasn't sure if they would have an opportunity. After the long kiss, Logan had escorted Marie back to her stateroom. Outside the door, he wanted to kiss her again, but Marie begged off, saying she had some work to do.

Like what kind of work?

Disappointed, Logan had returned to his own

stateroom, wondering if things would ever be the same, if they could someday become a couple again.

One thing he knew. He would never give her wedding ring to anyone else. If he had to keep the ring in his vault for the rest of his life, then that was the way it was going to be.

This morning, Logan was awakened by Jonas knocking on his door. The boy was showered, dressed, and ready to go. Mrs. Ping looked exhausted.

"Would you rather stay onboard to rest?" Logan asked her.

Mrs. Ping quickly took the offer.

It wasn't a long walk to the touristy part of Skagway, and they made it in good time, listening to Jonas babble about whatever popped into his little head. He even commented on the dirt and small rocks on the dusty sidewalk.

At an intersection, Marie looked at Logan. "Where do you want to go?"

"Anywhere he wants." Logan dipped his nose at Jonas. "Or it'll be a long day for us."

"I hear you."

As they walked forward, Logan felt that since Marie had asked him a question first, she had opened the door for them to have a conversation.

He'd take the opportunity until she closed the door on him again.

"How are you this morning?" Logan asked.

"Me?" Marie pointed to herself with her free hand.

"Yes. Did you sleep well?"

"You asked me that at breakfast."

"I did? I don't recall."

"You did. I was there first, remember, and you came into the dining room with Jonas and Mrs. Ping. As you sat down, you said, 'How are you this morning?' I said, 'I'm fine. And you?' And you said you would have preferred to sleep in all morning."

"Wow. You remembered our entire conversation?" Logan sped up his pace as Jonas dragged them forward. "All I remember is that first cup of coffee."

"You still put too much sugar in your coffee."

"That, I do." Logan knew he should cut back on putting too many sugar cubes into his coffee, but they were raw cane sugar, not processed.

"Well, I'm glad you gave Mrs. Ping a way out of this. We're basically chaperoning a spoiled brat—"

"I'm not a spoiled brat!" Jonas snapped.

Logan widened his eyes. Marie laughed.

"Ice cream!" Jonas pointed.

Marie checked her watch. "Not at eight thirty in the morning. Also you can get free ice cream onboard the ship if you wait until lunch."

"Free? He doesn't know what that is," Logan explained.

At the back of his mind, he appreciated how his wealth mattered very little to Marie. Her focus was somewhere else and on something else more tangible, perhaps.

Logan wished he had not divorced her. He had probably lost the most precious woman on earth.

How do I get her back, Lord Jesus? How?

The kiss on the top deck still lingered in his mind and heart. It wasn't the same as before, but it seemed to be a more mature, knowing kiss—if there was such a thing. Logan felt that they'd had more life experiences in the three years they had been apart, and had grown up.

Maybe this time it would last.

What would last, exactly?

"Something on your mind?" Marie asked unexpectedly.

They were approaching the ice cream shop.

"What Jonas wants, Jonas gets," Logan said.

"Is that what you've been thinking the last few minutes?"

"No," Logan confessed. "Not at all."

"Dare I even ask?"

"I was thinking about last night, and how we have both matured in three years. I think we're better people now."

"Better?" Marie paused. "I don't know if we can be *better* in our lives on earth, considering we drag around our sin nature even after we're saved in Jesus Christ."

"True. I guess I meant that we aren't as dull and insipid as we once were three years ago."

"Speak for yourself, Logan." Marie chuckled.

They entered the ice cream shop, crowded with wide-eyed kids and their befuddled parents. Someone remarked about not eating ice cream so early in the morning. Someone else said they were on vacation, as if that was an excuse.

"Are you getting anything?" Logan eyed the wall-to-wall list of items to choose from.

"I don't know," Marie replied.

"I want everything!" Jonas jumped up and down. "Daddy, buy this ice cream shop!"

Logan and Marie laughed. A few people in line joined in.

"Kids," someone said.

"We came all the way here to eat ice cream, can you believe it?" Logan remarked.

Several of the parents nodded. "Yeah. Might as well stay at home."

"Exactly what I thought." Logan inched forward in the line.

"I can't see the board, Daddy." Jonas had his arms straight up.

Logan lifted him to his shoulders. He wondered what good that would do, since Jonas could barely read, even though he could now see the board above all the other heads.

Marie was on her phone. Logan was about to confiscate it like she did his, when she showed the screen to Jonas.

"They have an app with photos of all the cups and cones," Marie explained. "You want to see what they can make you?"

Jonas nodded. His little index finger scrolled the page up, as if it was the most natural thing to do.

"When I was his age, I turned pages in a physical book," Logan said.

"I know. His digital generation is so many light years ahead of us," Marie replied.

"I want this...and this...and this..." Point. Scroll. Swipe.

When they reached the front of the line, the crowd did not thin out.

"I'll find a table," Marie said.

"Tell me what you want." Logan wondered if she...

"I always get the same thing."

So she hadn't changed. She still only ordered sorbet. "Any flavor?"

"Surprise me."

Surprise me? Now that surprised Logan. "Okay."

Some minutes later Marie was waiting, wiping a round table by the window that had just been vacated by a messy family. Logan arrived with more napkins on a tray of ice cream for him and Jonas, and sorbet for Marie.

"What did you get me?" Marie pointed to a chair for Jonas to sit on.

"Taste and see." Logan wanted to know if she liked it.

Before she responded, Marie glanced at the entrance to the ice cream shop. Logan's back was facing it, so he turned to look.

Aliyah and her entourage entered the ice cream shop.

"Abdul!" Jonas waved to his new friend.

Abdul nearly came over, but his mother held his hand tightly. She didn't smile. Her assistant was looking at a takeout menu. Behind them, Zaid stood guard.

Logan looked back to find Marie staring out of the window. There, by the roadside, were two familiar-looking men.

"Aren't those the men from last night?" Logan asked.

Marie didn't respond.

"Shall we thank God for the ice cream?" Jonas asked, preventing Logan's thoughts from wandering too far off.

They said a blessing over their ice cream and sorbet.

There was nothing to talk about. Ice cream was ice cream. Logan decided to ask Marie about her work.

"I suppose being a translator has its adventures," he said.

Instead of answering him, Marie said something odd. "When do you think the next Yukon train runs?"

"Why?" Logan asked.

"Maybe we could take Jonas on a train ride."

"Train is fun," Jonas said. "But not today. Today I'm a gold digger."

"What?" Logan was losing track of the scattered conversation.

"Mrs. Ping said if I get enough gold nuggets, I can be a Junior Ranger."

"What?"

Marie pulled out her cell phone. "I'll text her."

Logan finished his small scoop of ice cream. It had too much chocolate and sugar and fudge in it.

He wanted more. But the line was too long.

"Okay." Marie read her text. "Mrs. Ping forgot to tell us that if we take the little one to the Klondike Gold Rush Historical Park, he could earn his Junior Ranger badge."

"Where is this park?" Logan asked.

"I don't know. She sent me a link. One sec." Marie scrolled. "There's an activity center down the road from here. He could get his badge there. I think that's all it takes."

Logan stared at Jonas. Half the time he had no idea what coursed through that five-year-old. At that age, Logan wouldn't have given up a train ride to get a badge.

He wanted to say something to Marie, but she was looking out the window again. He followed her gaze. Out there, their new friends were walking toward a bench.

Three men, two women, and a lonely boy—not unlike Jonas. Logan wondered if the boy felt lonely sometimes, not having another kid to talk to. Maybe he and Jonas had become friends on account of that.

Logan wished he had more kids, for Jonas's sake.

Marie's phone vibrated on the table. She picked it up.

Logan almost said to her, "We're on vacation."

But when he saw her frowning at the message or email, he decided not to say anything.

Marie put away her phone. "Is it possible for you to take Jonas to the activity center? I have some work to do. I need to get back to the ship."

"No." Logan didn't know why that came out of his mouth.

"No?"

"No, please. You're going back to work next week. You'll be working the rest of the year. Let's save this time for our son."

"Says the person who tried to work through the salmon bake on Monday. Remember Juneau?" Marie said.

"Well... I learned my lesson. And now we're having family time—or what's left of it. He will never be five again. This is our time."

"This is our time," Marie echoed him. "All right. Work can wait."

"Thank you."

"No. Thank you." Marie reached across the small table and put her hand in his.

It was a small gesture, but it filled Logan's heart to overflowing.

CHAPTER EIGHTEEN

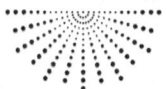

*H*anding Jonas over to Mrs. Ping at their stateroom door was the best thing Marie felt they could do for themselves this afternoon. A bona fide Junior Ranger now, Jonas himself wanted to spend the afternoon with Mrs. Ping—who had gotten herself a haircut and a perm while they had been in Skagway.

Mrs. Ping seemed happy to get Jonas back. "I missed you so much."

"I've only been gone a little bit." Jonas returned the hug. "What did you do all morning?"

"Well..." Mrs. Ping gently touched her hair with her hand.

"You got a haircut!" Jonas said.

"And a perm."

Everyone, except Logan, complimented Mrs. Ping on her new hair color. Logan didn't even bother to play along.

One of the things that Marie liked about Logan was how he'd tell it like it is. If he didn't like something, he would say it. No embellishment.

A dish you cooked tastes bad. That color is ugly on you. And so forth.

Rude as might be at times, Logan meant well, and that was how Marie chose to view it.

"I think we need alone time," he had said on their walk back to the ship for lunch. "We need to talk."

"What about the t-r-a-i-n?" Marie spelled it out for him.

"Train?" Jonas interjected their conversation. "I told you, next time."

Like father, like son.

In this particular case, Marie decided to tell Logan that she could not spend the afternoon with him. She couldn't tell him that she had to get back to her laptop, connect to her secure account at INTERPOL, and find out who Aliyah really was.

Marie had a feeling something wasn't right. Aliyah seemed to be a prisoner of some sort.

On the other hand, Marie might be wrong altogether.

She had to know.

And she couldn't know if Logan was around her all the time. He had no idea what Marie did for a living, and that secret had been the downfall of their marriage.

If she told him...

No.

"Time for a bath to wash away all that gold dust," Mrs. Ping said to Jonas.

He was rubbing his eyes.

"Maybe a nap after bath," Mrs. Ping said to Logan and Marie. "We might go to the playroom. If they're showing a movie at the theater, we might do that. I'll keep him until dinner. You two go do your own thing."

After Mrs. Ping closed the door, Logan waited for Marie to say something.

Marie assumed he wanted to know her decision about the "alone time" he had suggested.

"You're right," Marie said. "We both need alone time. I have some work to do. I'm sure you do, too. I'll see you at dinner?"

Logan didn't seem to visibly react too much, but Marie could see the disappointment in his eyes. He didn't reach for her hand or anything, but Marie had a feeling he wanted to.

She debated whether to give him a hug.

"You didn't answer my question in the ice-cream shop this morning," Logan said.

"What question?"

"I asked you about your translator job, and you replied about the Yukon train running."

"That. I don't usually talk about my job in public." Marie would have answered him had Aliyah's assistant—who spoke English—not walked into the shop at the moment that Logan had asked Marie the question.

The last thing Marie wanted them to know was that she was a translator. Although they wouldn't know what languages she spoke—they might have guessed it was a European language—Marie still did not want her cover blown.

What cover?

Marie closed her eyes. *I'm not working this week. I'm not working this week.*

"Are you tired?" Logan asked.

"A little bit." Marie stepped back. "I think I better go take a nap. You rest, too, and I'll see you at dinner."

Logan nodded. "And once again you did not answer my question about your job."

"I'm still doing the same thing I did five years ago." Marie took another step back. Her stateroom was down that way.

Logan didn't move from his spot. He didn't say anything.

Marie felt sorry for him. *Poor guy needs a hug.*

So she gave him a hug, wrapping her arms around him, and stroking his back. He relaxed under her arms.

In spite of everything he had and owned the world over, all he needed right now was a free hug.

Oh, the irony.

CHAPTER NINETEEN

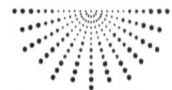

"*D*on't walk with me tonight because you feel sorry for me." Logan pushed the elevator button outside the dining room. He felt that Marie had come along only because she had to keep her word to walk with him this evening.

Dinner was over, and the ship was back at sea, cruising toward the next port of call. They should arrive in Ketchikan by morning.

"I know you want to talk," Marie said, stepping over the threshold. "I know you have questions."

"That you can't answer—or are not willing to." Oops. Logan cringed. He waited for Marie to spin around and walk away from his life.

She did not.

He was surprised.

They said nothing more to each other as they climbed the stairs to the upper deck, where they had been the night before. The wind picked up, flapping Logan's unbuttoned jacket, pulling him this way and that. The wind also spun around Marie's narrow ankle-length skirt, twisting it up and down her calves.

"Maybe we should go inside," Logan suggested.

Marie nodded.

The nearest door was to the piano lounge. There were people inside, drinking, laughing, talking. Someone was at the grand piano.

As they entered the area, a couple vacated their corner bench seat. It was tight space, but Marie nodded in that direction, so Logan went for it.

They settled into the corner, hip to hip.

"I don't know how we can talk here." Logan chuckled. "I have to turn my neck ninety degrees to see your face."

Marie glanced at her other shoulder, where a rather large, muscular man had wiggled himself into the seat next to her.

"Maybe we should leave," Logan whispered in her ear. "Do you want to try my balcony? We'll pile up with blankets and coats if it gets too windy."

Marie nodded.

Logan got up first, and pulled Marie to her feet. He decided not to let go of her hand as they made their way to his stateroom.

"We can order some snacks," Logan suggested.

"Oh, no. I'm too full." Marie touched her stomach. "Maybe mineral water, but that's all."

Logan nodded. Suddenly he remembered that his stateroom was a mess. He was sure the stewards had made his bed a second time while he was at dinner, but he had piles of paperwork and plugged-in laptop strewn all over his table.

Oh well.

"The reason I agreed to go to your room is that we've been married before to each other," Marie said.

"No need to explain. God already knows."

"I wanted it to be clear to *you* that I'm not asking for a reconciliation."

Logan was still holding Marie's hand. "I just want God's perfect will to be done for our family, especially for Jonas. I'm grateful that you agreed to take time out of your busy schedule to give him this birthday present. He won't forget it."

"You?"

"I won't forget it either. You're still the mother of my son." Logan unlocked his stateroom door.

Sure enough, the stewards had made his bed.

Everything looked nice and clean, except his messy workspace.

"Can't get away from work, huh?" Marie smiled. "Still printing out everything, I see."

"They make small and portable printers these days."

Marie stepped away from the door so that Logan could close it. "Ever heard of digital documents? Save a tree."

"I should, but I think better on paper." Logan opened the small refrigerator below a counter, where the stewards had put a bowl of fresh fruits. "Mineral water, you said?"

Marie nodded.

Logan handed her a small, cold bottle of mineral water and a glass. "Should I pour it for you?"

"I can do it myself." Marie thanked him for the water.

Logan led the way to the sliding glass door. Outside, the moon was out and the wind had subsided. Perhaps it was because each stateroom balcony was private, separated by a panel that acted like a windbreaker.

They stretched out on the lounge chairs.

"I suppose being a translator has its adventures," Logan said.

"Yeah, no dull moments." Marie seemed to wait for the next question.

Logan knew she wasn't going to volunteer any information. It had been like that for a while.

"I have a confession to make." Logan watched Marie's face. That got her attention.

"You're dying?"

"No. I'm as healthy as an Urquhart can be. It will take a lot to kill us."

Marie flinched a little bit.

"Are you okay?" Logan asked. Was it what he just said?

Marie didn't answer. She sipped her mineral water. Looked out into the night sea and sky and stars.

"I must tell you now, even if you'll hate me, and even if we've had a good time onboard this ship. I think you need to know." Logan was starting to feel better already even though he hadn't said what it was.

"Go on."

"Before we divorced, I hired a private investigator to follow you around Europe."

"Cost you a pretty fortune."

"You knew?"

"He didn't know how to hide. I almost invited him to have a cup of coffee just to make him feel at home. Next time, hire someone from Europe. He might blend in better."

Logan didn't know what to say except, "I'm sorry."

"I'm sorry, too, that we could not communicate," Marie said. "Tonight is your chance, Logan. Ask me anything. Maybe that will clear the air between us, and we can move forward as parents to Jonas."

After all these years, Logan was stumped. "How's your mom?"

"She's fine. My father's fine too, but he lost his sister last year."

"I'm sorry. Aunt Juliette?"

Marie nodded. "You know she was ill for a long time. In the end, the cancer took her."

"I'm very sorry."

"She's in heaven now, with her beloved husband. You remember they were married fifty years before he had the heart attack while working in his garden? He died in the middle of the flowers he had planted for his wife."

"They had many wonderful years together." It was all Logan could say.

"Many grandchildren," Marie added. "But my family is not really what you want to ask about, right?"

Logan crossed his legs. "I don't know what I want to know, really. I want us to be honest with each other, but we're not married anymore, and it doesn't seem like I have the right to ask you to tell me about the ninety percent of your life that I didn't know about when we were married."

"It's for the best."

Logan laughed. "That's what they all say. And then they spend the next three years with a hole in their lives, having let someone slip away."

"Is that how you feel?"

"You know our marriage vows. 'What God has put together, let no man put asunder.' That one?"

"It was a traditional vow."

"We chose it together."

"Yes, we did."

"And then we broke it. We broke our marriage."

"It's too late, Logan," Marie said. "We have both moved on."

Logan sat up and faced Marie. "Have we moved on? Are you seeing someone now?"

"No. You know my job. I travel a lot—too much, sometimes. I'm hardly in one place long enough to date anyone."

"I'm busy with work too. You were the last person I dated."

"Really?" Marie laughed. "I thought the other bazillionaires would have swarmed around you."

"They want to date my money, you mean?"

Marie stopped laughing.

"Did you know that you're the only person I've ever gone out with who didn't care about my money?"

"Was that why you married me?" Marie closed the cap on her empty mineral water bottle and placed it on the small table next to her.

Logan hadn't noticed it until now, but she had kept her small clutch purse next to her hip instead of on the table, which had space for that little purse.

He wondered what was in the purse, but he wasn't going to ask. The last time he looked into her purse, a little Glock stared back at him. However, he doubted that the captain of this cruise ship would allow armed passengers onboard.

He sighed. There was so much he didn't know about Marie.

"I married you because..." Logan walked over to Marie and gently pulled her to her feet. "You saw me for me only, we were good with each other, we both love God, and I knew that I could never love another like I loved you."

"But we're divorced."

"I don't know what happened, and I wish we never did."

"You were jealous, Logan," Marie reminded him. "You thought I was having an affair. You sent that bungling PI to track me down. What did he tell you?"

"Nothing."

"Exactly." Marie let go of his hand. She stepped toward the railing. "Because there was no one else. However, because you sent the PI, you put yourself and Jonas in danger."

Logan sat up. He couldn't believe it. "It took you three years to tell me that?"

"We took care of it."

"*We* who?"

"I can't say, but trust me when I tell you that your PI put our son in danger when he went out there asking people about me on behalf of a then toddler."

"I—uh..." Logan didn't remember telling the PI to keep a lid on who had sent him. He certainly didn't recall asking the man to use their little boy as bait.

Logan drew a deep breath. He walked back and forth on the small balcony. "All I tried to do was to find out if...if you were..."

He couldn't finish his sentence.

"Someday I will tell you everything," Marie said. "For now, know that when the PI tracked me down at a trade show I attended, it put you and Jonas on the radar. That took months and months of work to undo."

"Radar? Whose radar? How?"

"I can't say. Suffice to tell you that your PI talked too much to anyone and everyone, even putting himself in danger. I'm glad you fired him."

"Wait. Danger? He said it was like a vacation."

Marie's eyebrows rose. "Of course he would say that. He was nearly killed. He didn't tell you?"

"No. Come to think of it, he said he had another assignment following the job I sent him to do, so we didn't see each other until six months later." The new information made Logan realize that Marie was definitely not only a translator.

"During which time he was probably all healed up."

"I don't know what to think, Marie. I did what I thought was the best thing to do."

"A marriage is based on trust."

"And we have too little—or none—of it." Logan sighed.

For all practical purposes, everything was water under the bridge now. The only thing that had between them was a small handful of happy moments, including the birth of their only child. Beyond that, what was left of their relationship?

"If you want to find me next time, call this person." Marie retrieved a card from her purse, and handed it to Logan.

"Mendenhall Security. No contact name?"

"She's all over the place. If you're looking for me, call that number. Ask for Espy." It was time to tell Logan at least one other person he could trust for the safety of their family.

Esperanza did not work for INTERPOL. She was a freelance security specialist who ran her own company, Mendenhall Security, although Marie had known her long before she started the company with the money her husband had left her after he was murdered. Marie met Esperanza for the first time on the project that had ended three years before, and Esperanza was like an older sister to her.

"You want me to find you?" Logan asked.

"No, but in case you need assurance or something."

"Or another hug." Logan's voice was so low he didn't know if Marie heard him.

She reached for him.

Yeah, she heard me.

She patted his shoulder. "You'll be fine."

Bummer. No hug.

"If Espy says I'm busy, you need to believe her. You got it?" Marie's voice wasn't harsh, but it seemed like she wanted Logan to agree with her.

"Okay. Are you undercover or something?"

Marie laughed. "I'm surprised you haven't already remarried."

So quickly had she changed the subject.

"You'd think that your cousin Jared would have lined up a whole host of potential wives for you," Marie said.

Logan was surprised at the statement. "I don't think so. I'm a one-woman man."

"Is that right?"

"I found her, and I lost her." Logan tapped the railing. "Such is life."

Such is life.

CHAPTER TWENTY

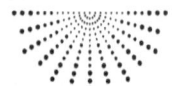

*K*etchikan was one of those unique towns that had a forest and a glacier nearby, and spawning salmons swimming upstream in between. The June weather was mild, just the way Marie liked it, but she could see that it did nothing for Jonas, who was tired of the uphill walk to a park.

Yes, a park.

It was by the salmon hatchery, and a creek was supposed to run through it, but Marie was no longer confident they were going to make it.

Jonas had been whining since they left Mrs. Ping on the ship. She had other plans that didn't seem to include Alaska much.

But it wasn't about Mrs. Ping.

"What's the matter, Son?" Logan kept asking, to no avail.

Marie had no idea how to handle it. She quietly prayed.

Something is wrong with this child today and I have no clue, Lord.

She wondered if she would have been a better mother now if she hadn't left Jonas. However, she had no choice. She could blame Logan for that. Yes, she could.

If Logan had not sent that dreadful PI to follow her around in Europe some three years before, the terrorists she had been tracking wouldn't have discovered that she had a young son in America whom they could leverage to get INTERPOL off their backs.

Fortunately, INTERPOL and the FBI had worked together to create a false narrative to throw off their assailants. A decoy stood in for Marie. A female agent, who looked sort of like Marie, took her place. Unfortunately, she had to beat up Logan's PI. It was part of the coverup.

After that, Marie knew that she had to let Logan and Jonas go, if only to keep them alive.

What Logan didn't know was that she had paid out of her own pocket to hire her friend to send someone to Atlanta to keep an eye on Jonas for the next six to nine months until the danger had passed.

"I want to go back to the ship," Jonas suddenly declared.

The family hike ground to a halt right there on the uphill sidewalk. Every now and then a vehicle drove by. The fenced houses around them were quiet. Above them was another clear day in Alaska.

"We're only a few minutes away from the hatchery," Logan said.

"I don't care." Jonas pouted.

Whine, whine.

Marie couldn't stand it. "Say exactly what you are thinking right now, Jonas, or we keep walking."

"Yes, we need to finish what we started," Logan added.

"I want to go to the playroom." Jonas tugged at Logan's arm.

"Note that he's not tugging at my arm," Marie said. "Because I won't let him."

Logan frowned. "Let's argue later. We have a spoiled brat on our hands right now."

"On your hands, not mine." Marie felt sorry saying it.

Logan knelt down in front of Jonas. They were at eye level with each other. "Jonas, almost every passenger left the ship to go on excursions. There is probably no one in the playroom right now. When we go back, I'm sure your new friend will be there."

Jonas's eyes lit up. "Really? So if we go back right now, they will be there?"

"I meant after we have all finished our adventures here, and it's time to sail." Logan was still on his knees.

"When is that?"

"Tonight. We sail after dinner."

"So late."

Logan nodded. "We get to spend all day here with Mommy. We only have a few days left with her, and then she has to go back to work."

Jonas's eyes widened. He stared at Marie. He looked like he was about to cry. He ran to Marie, wrapped both arms around her waist, and said something muffled.

Marie stroked his hair.

My son, whom I have left to save his life.

Why is life so unfair, Lord? Why can't I have my job and a family too?

Mother and son hugged for a while.

Logan cleared his throat. "How about we go back to town and walk around. There's Creek Street. Maybe we can get some ice cream—"

"Whoopee!" Jonas detached himself from Marie, and jumped up and down.

"After lunch," Logan added.

"No! Now!" Jonas clenched his fists.

"What have we produced?" Marie asked Logan. She glanced at her watch. It was barely ten o'clock. "We had breakfast, so technically he's not getting i-c-e on an empty stomach."

"Then again, if we give in, he's not mature enough to differentiate the logic and reasoning behind our assent now."

"Indeed. That means he might try this again on us later, and it would not have the same results. Or would it?"

Standing in between his parents, Jonas made a face. "Are you talking about me?"

"Who else would we be talking about?" Logan asked. "Do you see another brat around?"

"I thought Brad is my middle name," Jonas said.

Marie rolled her eyes.

"You see I can't do this alone." Logan reached for Marie's hand. "Seems to me that it takes two parents to usher this brat into adulthood."

For some reason, Marie didn't move nor did she say a word. Logan took another step toward her. He was close enough to kiss her on the cheek.

Until Jonas wiggled in between them. He looked up at his parents. "Did we forget ice cream or what?"

CHAPTER TWENTY-ONE

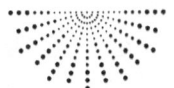

reek Street was overrun with tourists, who probably looked like scurrying mobs of ants from afar. The wooden boardwalks at the edge of the gurgling stream seemed to be able to hold that much weight, although Logan had to navigate through the crowd, with Jonas and Marie behind him in single file.

Logan glanced back every now and then to make sure they were still there. He slowed down at one point, and let Marie walk ahead first. Jonas was still in between them, chatting away about whatever it was. Logan hadn't paid any attention.

His eyes were on the back of Marie's head and her shoulders, trying to remember moments in their lives together that he had missed so much.

It had been three long years.

Since they were older now, couldn't they talk through whatever differences they had?

Then again, sometimes people fell away from each other and never returned to where they once were.

Lord, please don't let us be like that.

I want a second chance, if it's possible.

"Where are we going?" Marie glanced back.

"Away from this crowd," Logan said over Jonas's head. "I think if we turn a corner there to where the shops are..."

"That seems counterintuitive." Marie pointed toward the bay. "You see a second wave of cruise ships are docking now."

"Yeah, I know. Maybe we can slip into the shops in between the waves."

Marie nodded.

Logan had no idea if he would be right or not, but he gave Marie credit for not arguing with him.

As a kid with a short memory, Jonas hadn't asked to return to the ship, although they could have taken left turn at the stairs ahead, and walk back to the ship.

Jonas's mind seemed to be sidetracked by the idea of eating ice cream.

The crowd started to clear as the road bifurcated.

"Take the road less traveled by," Logan told Marie.

"And that will make all the difference," she said.

Jonas suddenly waved. "Abdul! Abdul!"

In front of what looked like a souvenir shop some thirty feet away was Jonas's new friend, together with his escorts. They were walking into the shop.

His friend didn't seem to hear nor see him.

Jonas pulled Logan's hand. "Let's go!"

"What about ice cream?" Logan asked.

"Later. I want a toy."

Marie sighed. Logan shrugged.

They entered the souvenir store. Logan was tall enough to look over the heads of the customers in the shop. He spotted Abdul and his mother by a barrel of rocks. He took Jonas there.

Marie tagged along. She seemed to be glancing this way and that.

"Go browse if you want," Logan said. "I'll stay with Jonas."

Jonas and Abdul were busy comparing small rocks in the barrel. They each filled a little satchel with them. According to the sign, the rocks sold by the pound.

Pound? Logan chuckled.

Standing behind Abdul was his mother and her friend. Behind them were two bodyguards—or whoever they were.

Logan wasn't the least bit curious, but he thought that might be a good conversation starter tonight when he and Marie walked after dinner—if she was still up to doing it.

He hadn't always thought of himself as observant, but Logan remembered seeing three men escorting these women by the pool on the ship a few days ago. It was probably nothing.

He turned around to see what Marie was doing. She was checking out some Matryoshka nesting dolls on a glass counter.

Logan smiled.

He turned around to ask Jonas if he wanted one—

And he wasn't there at the rock barrel.

Neither were Abdul and his entourage.

What on earth?

"Jonas?" Logan's head snapped this way and that as he scanned the shop. He could not see anyone wearing hijabs over their heads. Neither did he see the two men.

Marie was at his side in almost a flash. "What's going on? Where's Jonas?"

"I don't know. He was here a minute ago and I looked back and he's gone."

Marie's eyes grew fierce. "This store has two entrances. You take that one, and I take this. You have your cell phone?"

Logan nodded. "Meet you back here at the rock barrel in five minutes?"

"Or we call 911."

Logan prayed it wouldn't get to that. He rushed through the crowd, calling out his son's name, hoping he didn't look like a madman.

Her remembered Marie's fierce look. And he felt like a failure. He couldn't even keep an eye on his son for a minute.

"Jonas!" He heard Marie's voice from the other end of the store, and he understood what she might be feeling. There was no time for etiquette when a five-year-old child was missing.

Logan waved to a couple of store sales clerks to ask if they had seen Jonas. He wished he had taken a photo of his boy before they left the ship, so that he could have shown these people what his son looked like.

"Blonde, big eyes, blue striped tee-shirt, hiking

pants, bright yellow hiking boots." It was all the information Logan could give.

They shook their heads. "Only when we saw you come in with him."

Logan had no time to rehash that he only turned around for a split second. Maybe even less time than that.

Between the two of them, they had covered the shop. Logan was at one of the entrances now.

Lord Jesus, help me find my son.

Help us find our son!

Outside on the sidewalk, Logan wished he had put a GPS tracker on his son. He saw a bench. He asked the two tourists sitting there if they could get up.

"My five-year-old son vanished from the store and we're looking for him," he explained as he leapt on the vacated bench, quickly scanning the crowd along the boardwalk by the river.

And there he was.

Surrounded by Abdul's mother and their group.

Logan jumped off the bench. "Thank you!"

He ran as he called Marie—who suddenly appeared by his side before the call went through.

"He's down there," Logan said, trying to remain calm. "With Abdul's family."

"Thank God!" Marie kept up with Logan as they rushed down the boardwalk.

Jonas and Abdul were leaning over the railing, looking at the river.

"Here fishy! Fishy!" Jonas's hand was stretched out.

With one giant stride, Logan yanked him off the railing. "You could fall over!"

"Dad, you're scaring the fish. Inside voice, please." Jonas seemed oblivious to the drama he had put his parents through.

"Next time, before you go anywhere, you need to let Mommy and Daddy know," Logan lectured Jonas. "We thought we lost you at the store."

"We came to see the fish." Jonas nodded to Abdul, and Abdul nodded back.

Truly, it was the adults' fault—Abdul's mother, the other woman, and those three men. Logan didn't even want to look at their faces right now. He was a bit angry that the strangers had taken his son out of the store without his permission.

Marie smiled, but Logan could see it was forced.

"Thank you for taking care of our son," she said nicely to the women.

One woman turned to the other, who translated what Marie said into a Middle Eastern language that Logan didn't speak. It sounded like Arabic, but he couldn't be sure.

The first woman smiled and said something in her own language.

The second woman standing behind her translated for Marie and Logan. "Her excellency says we thought you knew your boy walked with us."

"However, he hadn't paid for his bag of rocks." Logan pointed to what Jonas held in his hand.

"We paid for it," the second woman said.

"I didn't see you go to the checkout," Logan said.

The woman pointed to one of the two men with them. "He took care of it."

"I should reimburse you." Logan reached for his wallet.

The man held up his hand. "No need."

Logan noted then that not only did the man understand English, but he also spoke in British English, not American. One more thing to bring up to Marie tonight.

Marie.

Logan didn't know why he kept thinking of Marie, especially when she was standing next to him. He felt like he was going to lose her as soon as this cruise was over.

Would he lose her for real this time?

Marie was holding Jonas's hand, as if not wanting to let go.

I feel the same too, if that's what she's feeling.

"So are we getting ice cream?" Jonas asked, as if nothing had happened at all.

"I could use some right now," Logan declared.

"Me too." Marie laughed.

But it was a nervous laughter.

CHAPTER TWENTY-TWO

*A*fter lunch in Ketchikan, they had returned to the ship. Neither Marie nor Logan was up to taking any water tour of the surrounding inlets, or going to see the bald eagles, or returning to the salmon hatchery. Marie was sure they'd all be back in Alaska again someday, and they'd do all that next time.

Right now, Marie had a feeling of déjà vu, like she had to protect Jonas all over again. Perhaps she was overreacting. Who'd expected that a five-year-old would sneak out of a shop with an entire group of people?

Under Logan's nose!

Hovering or not, Marie sat by Jonas's bedside as

he napped that afternoon in her stateroom. She insisted on keeping him with her there.

She didn't have any of her gear or equipment from work with her. The only thing she had was a deactivated Radio Frequency Identification tracker on a bracelet in her purse. She could, technically, put it on Jonas's ankle—if he would cooperate and not take it off, and if Mrs. Ping didn't question what it was. Perhaps she'd put it on Jonas before the next excursion and hide it under his socks.

Unfortunately, the RFID tracker had a short range. If someone took Jonas out of the next town, they might not be able to find him.

Marie wished she had brought her GPS tracker with her. However, she had not expected any drama on board the ship or at any of the small tourist towns they were visiting along the Inside Passage in Alaska. Seriously.

Earlier, Logan had also wanted Jonas in his cabin, but an inopportune business phone call canceled his plan, and Marie got the child.

After the nap, Marie accompanied Jonas to the playroom, where they met up with Abdul and his mother, Aliyah, again.

Marie wasn't sure how to address her, but the woman had not given her an indication of her position in her own society, so there was no title for Marie to use. Even though she had heard the assistant saying Your Highness, that hadn't been translated for Marie.

So Aliyah it was.

Once again, she wasn't alone. The assistant was behaving like a handler. Never smiling, always looking uptight, her job seemed to be to make sure Aliyah and her son stayed safe.

Or didn't wander off on their own.

They were in American waters right now, and the ship would sail down the Inside Passage for a feast of glaciers the next day. After one day down the inlets, they would arrive in Victoria on Friday.

Canada.

Marie wasn't sure whether it would make any difference if they had been in either the United States or Canada. A child abduction was a child abduction no matter which country they were in.

Marie yawned on the way to dinner. She wondered if she should have slept while Jonas had napped earlier, but she had been too uptight to close her eyes then.

Jonas was skipping happily, with Mrs. Ping by his side.

Marie didn't see Logan anywhere.

She missed him. The family didn't feel complete without Logan for some reason.

When they were seated, Logan had still not arrived.

Marie texted him.

He texted back, saying he had overslept, but he was on his way.

Marie waited anxiously until Logan arrived.

"Missed me?" Logan asked. It seemed that his question was directed at everyone, but he was looking at Marie in particular.

Marie didn't answer him. She didn't want to sound forward or give away a secret or two about how she still felt about him.

But yes, I missed you.

CHAPTER TWENTY-THREE

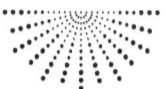

They almost met again in Logan's stateroom for their private conversation, but he confessed that his room was even messier than before, and he had hung the Do Not Disturb sign on his door, thereby preventing the stewards from making his bed or cleaning up his bathroom.

"In other words, you're saying that it's a pig sty," Marie said as the elevator door closed.

They were the only people in it. They had left dinner late, and everyone else had gone on to their after-dinner activities.

"So can we go to your room?" Logan sounded pleading.

"You want to see my cabin."

"Because it's bound to be cleaner than mine." Logan lowered his voice. "We can't talk about things on the top deck or in any open area. I've been doing some investigating..."

Investigating? "No, Logan."

"I meant research. Okay, I googled. Some things didn't make sense."

"The whole world doesn't make sense sometimes."

"Just give me an hour. If you still don't think I'm onto something, then kick me out and I'll be out of your way."

The elevator door opened to their floor. Standing there, about to enter it, was Zaid, one of Aliyah's bodyguards. He was dressed in a long-sleeved charcoal shirt, buttoned up to his neck. He had on a pair of slacks.

And military boots.

Marie made eye contact with him. He nodded to her. There was a hint of respect in his nod, as if...

No. Nobody knows who I am.

Zaid held the door, and waited for Marie and Logan to step out of the elevator.

"Thank you, Zaid," Marie said quietly.

His eyebrows rose.

Yes, I know your name.

When the elevator door closed, Logan said, "Hmm. You know his name."

"They mentioned it in the playroom."

"The playroom, huh?"

"Yeah. We should take turns accompanying Jonas there. I'm not the only one on parent duty onboard the ship." Marie led the way toward her stateroom.

"What's Abdul's mother's name?"

Marie didn't answer Logan until they were safely inside her stateroom. She kicked off her heels, and placed her purse in the safe.

"Aliyah," she finally answered. "She introduced herself to me as such, but her assistant called her Your Highness."

"No kidding. The plot thickens." Logan sat down on the sofa, untied his shoelace, and pulled out his phone.

"There's no plot." Marie asked him if he wanted some water. He shook his head.

"Isn't there?" Logan motioned for Marie to sit down. "I made a list."

"I thought you were working all afternoon on your merger issues."

"That, too, but this was bothering me, so I thought about it. I didn't finish because I fell asleep."

"At least you had a nap. I was watching Jonas the entire time, praying for God's protection for us." Marie sat down on the other side of the coffee table in a small armchair.

"I should pray more," Logan said.

"To be honest, I'm trying not to read too much into what happened this morning in Ketchikan. So I turned around for a split second, and our five-year-old wandered out of the store with his new friend Abdul and his family."

"There were only two exits, and somehow we missed both of them."

"We made a mistake looking inside the store. One of us should've gone outside."

"Maybe. Instead we both looked inside the store, so by the time we reached the doors, they had gone down the boardwalk."

"They didn't go too far. Only to where the bridge was."

"To see the fish." Logan rubbed his bare chin. "However, what made me upset the rest of it. When we went to get Jonas, what did they say?"

"Nothing."

"Exactly. It was as though they saw nothing wrong for a child to walk with them out of the store."

"They have three bodyguards, although only

two seemed to have gone out with them." Marie wondered what the third bodyguard was doing. It was none of her business—unless they made it her business.

"Those were bodyguards? How did you know?" Logan asked.

"You remember the second day when we were out at sea? Mrs. Ping and I took Jonas to the pool? I was sitting poolside when their whole group showed up. There were three men, two women, and one boy."

"And the boy was about the same size and height as Jonas. If you put baseball caps on them, I bet you couldn't tell them apart."

"Not from a distance, no," Marie agreed. "Up close, a stranger can probably tell that Jonas has a chubby face and blue eyes, and Abdul's eyes are dark brown and his face is more tanned."

"I need to get Jonas out in the sun more often. He prefers to play in his playroom at home. It took lot of effort to get him to the backyard to play soccer."

"Even if he gets out in the sun, you can still tell the kids apart. However, I get your point." Marie wondered where Logan was going with this.

He was a businessman, but a savvy one at that.

He had an eye for details, yes, but did she want him to continue with this?

She could not tell him what she had found out from her office in France. It might be premature yet. She was waiting for them to contact FBI and MI5 to get more details. She had sent them enough photos and videos for them to squeeze through their facial recognition software.

If she told Logan all of that, he would begin to question her again. It was best if he didn't know.

Or was it?

"I want to believe that it was a genuine error," Logan said. "But what kind of a mother—or parent, for that matter—would take someone else's child along with them without parental consent, and then not apologize for it?"

"Maybe their language barrier prevented them from apologizing."

"You don't think it's cultural."

Marie shook her head. "Every culture has moms and dads. It's normal for us to protect our children. They know that."

"Exactly."

"What do you mean?"

"I suspect they took Jonas with them on purpose."

"Now you're speculating."

"Am I?"

"Don't go all paranoid on me, Logan."

"It was so quick, though." Logan crossed his feet on the coffee table and leaned back against the sofa.

Marie remembered how she used to cuddle next to him while he was relaxed like that. They'd watch TV or listen to music or the news. She didn't care what they were listening to or watching as long as she was with him.

Those days were long gone now.

Although the danger was over now, Marie wondered if new danger was rolling in.

Marie hadn't been assigned to the Middle East in several years, so she was quite sure it had nothing to do with that. After she was done with it, they kept her in France, chasing after a French terrorist, not Middle Eastern.

Granted, that project was not over, but Marie had asked to be removed from the project after they captured Molyneux's associates in Tel Aviv. Once the team returned to Europe, her Arabic linguistics abilities were no longer needed.

The multinational effort to hunt for Molyneux and her terrorist organization went on, but Marie's part in all of that was over. They had enough French speakers, and she could go home.

Perfect timing to take a break in Alaska with her son.

And ex-husband.

He seemed to be staring at her.

"Why are you looking at me like that?" Marie asked.

"Your mind is somewhere else," Logan said. "I can always tell. Or could, anyhow. If I didn't know you any better, I would say that you know more about Abdul's family than you let on."

"More speculating."

"Am I? You told me that Abdul's family had three bodyguards. What could possibly happen on a cruise ship?"

Marie didn't want to break the news to Logan that many things could happen on a cruise ship— murders and suicides, people falling overboard, to name just a few. Of course, there were less dramatic problems like food poisoning and fire.

"To be sure, we're not always on a cruise ship, yes?" Marie countered. "Whenever we go on excursions, we're on land."

"We were in Ketchikan. I think we're in good hands with the authorities if something happens on US soil."

"We'll be in Victoria on Friday, but I'm sure Canadian law enforcement is reliable too." Marie made a mental not to find out who to contact once they reached the island—in case anything happened.

Nothing is going to happen.

This is a simple no-drama vacation.

Marie chuckled. *Yeah, keep telling yourself that.*

"What's funny?" Logan asked. "What are you not telling me?"

"What am I not telling you?"

Logan dropped his feet onto the plush carpet, and leaned forward. When he did that, his eyebrows rose.

Marie had seen that look before. He was getting serious.

"When my PI gave me a report of what he found in Europe, he said that you worked for the US State Department."

"I work where I'm paid. If a diplomat or attaché asks for my translation services, I will work for them—if they pay me well and the assignment doesn't go against my personal principles. It's a job, Logan."

"Why did you carry a gun then?" Logan asked. "Do translators carry weapons as part of their work?"

"Some of us carry for our personal protection."

Marie wondered whether Logan's PI saw more than they had thought.

That day, three years before, her decoy had carried a gun. How would Marie disclose that fact without also sharing more about what she had been doing? Even a small amount of information could cause Logan to ask more questions.

Therefore, she could not tell him that she had been deep undercover that week when Vienna had been attacked, that they were chasing leads across Europe, trying to prevent another Vienna.

"Someday, when I'm retired, we will have a chat about all that. However, as I recall, I did not carry a gun during that particular week when I ran into your PI. Clearly, he was mistaken. It wasn't me."

"Another person who looked like you?"

Yes, the same one who beat up that PI. Another thing Marie could not tell Logan. Not right now.

"Whether you trust me or not, we have a problem at this time," Logan said.

"We don't know if your suspicions about Abdul's family are correct."

Logan shook his head. "Tell me you don't worry about Jonas."

"I worry." It was a confession, but Marie could not take it back.

"Then why does it look like you're brushing off the matter?"

"I'm not." Marie felt like she should tell him to leave her room now. "If you called this meeting so that we can get into an argument, then you're destroying any morsel of post-divorce friendship we might have."

"I'm only asking if you cared that our son was almost abducted this morning." Logan didn't raise his voice. He seemed genuinely unsure about what he was seeing.

"I told you I'm not making light of the situation. I totally care. But we need to be careful not to jump the gun and cause an unnecessary international incident."

"Like what?"

"Like accusing a foreign princess of attempting to abduct a five-year-old boy who merely followed them down the boardwalk to look at salmon swimming upstream."

"A princess?" Logan's eyes widened.

"I told you they called her Your Highness."

"I heard you, but it's not registering until now."

"Well, I'm not sure, but I'm guessing she might very well be one."

"When it comes to my own son, I don't trust anyone, even kings, queens, and heads of states."

Logan closed his eyes. Rubbed his temples. "Maybe you're right. I might have overreacted."

"I don't want you to talk to the bodyguards or approach Aliyah or her assistant. That would raise suspicions. We just need to find out what they're up to. I'm calling in favors, and I will let you know what they find. Okay?"

"Favors? What kind of favors?"

"Friends back home," Marie explained.

"Home as in France." Logan's shoulders sagged. "Somewhere in my heart I wished that we had made it work. I was so angry with you for leaving Jonas and me. You had been gone for months without letting me know where you were. Could you blame me for hiring the PI to find out if you were...if you were—I mean..."

"If I were having an affair? The answer is no. I had no time for such nonsense. Besides, I could only love..." Marie cleared her throat.

"Go on."

She didn't.

"Would you like to order snacks?" She asked instead.

"Don't change the subject. Besides, we already ate dinner and desserts."

Marie got up. "I need some fresh air."

She unlocked the balcony door. When she

opened it, she heard the swooshing of the Atlantic waves mixed in with the noisy wind, which blew in droplets of rain against her face.

She closed the sliding glass door. "Raining outside."

Logan's face reflected on the glass door. There were lines of sadness across his face, his eyes droopy. He reminded Marie of Jonas.

Like father, like son.

Marie turned around. "Please don't whine like Jonas."

Logan laughed. "Do I look like I am?"

"Your face looks like you're about to."

"Give me more credit than that. I'm thirty-five, not five!" Logan walked back to the sofa. He put on his shoes.

Marie didn't want him to leave, but it was for the best.

"I wish we could be more than friends, but we've been there, done that, and it didn't work out," Logan said. "I'm sorry I was pushy about the incident this morning. I'm probably just paranoid after that...uh."

"After what?" Marie placed her hands on her hips. "After what?"

"It was a while ago, and I'm sure it was nothing."

"A while ago when?"

Logan picked up his phone. "I'll email you what I found about Abdul's family."

"Don't change the subject."

"Touché."

Marie grabbed his arm. "Seriously, Logan. Is this about Jonas? Why didn't you hire security? This is your only son!"

Marie knew she had to backtrack later. She herself could have asked for continued security, but she had thought the danger was over.

"Whoa. Slow down." Logan held her hand. "If you must know..."

"Yes, I must know."

"Then sit down and I'll tell you about it."

CHAPTER TWENTY-FOUR

"*O*ne year ago? Now you tell me?" Marie's voice was rising. She paced the carpeted floor barefooted. "Someone broke into Jonas's bedroom and tried to kidnap him and you never said a word for one year?"

"Calm down, honey." Logan felt halfway between bad that he had to tell his ex-wife what happened to their son and good that he had finally gotten it off his chest.

"Don't you *honey* me." Marie stopped at the back of an armchair. "I wish you had told me before we boarded this ship."

"What would you have done?"

"Brought extra security, for example." She

placed her hands on the top of the chair's backrest. Her fingers dug into the leather.

Was it Logan's imagination, or did Marie's painted fingernails look like fangs?

"One year ago." Marie sighed. "That was long after we thought it was over."

"What was over? Who thought what was over?"

Marie didn't say.

Logan recalled all the questions of his own that had gone unanswered for six years. "If we keep more secrets between us, how can we come together to help our son? I told you everything, but you told me nothing. It's not fair, Marie. I can't do this with you this way."

"I have sworn not to talk about my work." Marie came around the chair and sat down. "I have one more assignment, and then I'm quitting."

"You're quitting what?"

"My job."

"Which one? Your translator job or the one you can't talk about?"

"They're the sa—I can't tell you."

"Were you trying to tell me they were the *same* job?"

Marie didn't respond.

"See what I mean?" Logan threw up his arms. "This is why we fought and argued a lot. You know me, but I don't know you."

"There's not a lot I can tell you, truly."

"Tell me enough inasmuch as it concerns Jonas. We will cross the other bridges after you retire—or quit—from whatever it is you've been doing behind my back for the last six years."

Marie closed her eyes. "I can tell you this much. Until two years ago, I translated for the State Department. While traveling around the Middle East, I was also their eyes and ears in meetings and conferences."

Eyes and ears?

Like a spy?

Logan didn't say a word but he was wondering how he never knew that Marie had been a spy. Still, she hadn't come right out and say it until now.

Eyes and ears.

Logan shook his head. "Was it dangerous?"

"Not if you're trained."

The other shoe dropped.

"Trained? So you're not just a translator?"

"Many ordinary people in various professions are sometimes called to help the government in times of war. You know that back in the World War

II era, even Julia Child—the world-renowned chef —was asked to listen in."

"Are we at war, Marie?"

Marie shrugged. "We're always at war. The point is, I was in the middle of an assignment, when your bungling PI waltzed in, brandishing photos of our son and me to everyone."

Logan's heart dropped. "I put you in danger."

"Yes, you did. I was reassigned after that, but the enemies went to Atlanta to track down the boy in the photo."

"Our son. I put our son in danger."

Marie stopped him from berating himself. "I paid Espy to send someone from Mendenhall Security to Atlanta to keep an eye on Jonas."

"I had no idea." Logan drew a deep breath. "It must have cost a fortune."

"What is the price of our son's head?"

Logan was taken aback by the question.

Marie sat down. "The good news was that after nine months, we—they—caught the bad guys, and so Jonas wasn't in danger anymore at that time."

Logan left the sofa. He sat down on the carpet in front of Marie's armchair. "I wish you had told me. We could have dealt with it together."

"I wasn't sure how normal you could act. I couldn't risk it."

"I think I would've freaked out."

"See what I mean." Marie ran her palm over his hair. "Both of you had to go about your daily business as normal as possible."

"Unfortunately, a year after that something happened." Logan rested his hand on one of Marie's knees. She didn't protest.

In fact, she placed her hand over his. "I wish I were there."

"We couldn't find you. I fired the PI, and I wasn't about to try again. I reported the break-in and attempted abduction to the local police. They somehow contacted the FBI and then next thing I knew, two agents showed up at my office."

"What were their names?"

"I can't remember, but I'm sure my secretary does. I'll ask her tomorrow if you must know."

"Let me know their names." Marie sighed. "Someone tried to harass us when Jonas was two years old. Then someone else entered your house when he was four years old. And here we are."

Us.

She said "harass us."

Logan almost felt like they were a family again.

"I wonder if it's related to my work," Marie said. "Or yours. Do you have enemies?"

"You mean like business rivals or competitors?" Logan couldn't imagine that any of his business associates would be criminal elements. "We have those all the time."

"Are they mean-spirited enough to try to disturb your family in any form?"

Logan shrugged. "What can I say about human nature? Sin is sin is sin is sin."

"Indeed. So it could be my work then. I will make some phone calls. Make all these go away."

"Is that all it's going to take?" Logan asked.

"I don't know."

"Did we forget that ultimately God is in control of our lives?"

"And that He will protect us and keep us safe." Marie sniffled. "Thank you for the reminder."

"This morning, in my quiet time with God, I read Psalm 61:3. May I read it to us now?" Logan reached for his phone.

Marie nodded.

Logan swiped his phone and read the verse.

For You have been a shelter
for me,
A strong tower from the
enemy.

"I have been camping out on this verse for a while," Logan explained. "Today, I started praying this verse for our family. Little did I know we were going to need it within twenty-four hours."

"God's Word never returns void. Look up Proverbs 18:10, please."

Logan did. "Another verse about God sheltering us. 'The name of the Lord is a strong tower; the righteous run to it and are safe.' You like that verse?"

"Whenever I'm in—hmm... Let's just say whenever I'm at work, God has been my protector."

"Has been?"

"So far. He will continue to protect me, to be sure."

Logan detected a hesitancy. "But you're tired of the job."

"Of my career, really. I think I need a change of pace. Maybe I need a sabbatical."

Logan smiled. "How about taking a sabbatical in Atlanta? Stay in our own five-star hotel. Any room you want, including the penthouse. Free chauffeurs service twenty-four seven. And a very active five-year-old concierge. When would you like to check in?"

Marie chuckled. "You're funny."

"I've always been funny, but maybe I want to be more than that to you."

Marie cleared her throat. "We were discussing our son's safety."

"Right. Right." Logan chided himself for forgetting that. Truth be told, he wasn't forgetting all that. But sitting here at Marie's feet...

Too close.

Yet he felt totally at home. Like he was meant to be there with her.

"I miss you, Marie," he blurted.

Truth was better told just the way it was, unvarnished, untamed, uncovered.

"I'm sorry for the danger I put you in," Marie said. "I had to stay away, hoping that maybe they would leave you two alone, but they didn't."

"I'm partly to blame for that. I wish I never hired the PI. He cost me a fortune."

"What's done is done, as my mother says."

"If we could do it over, would you have left?" Logan didn't know why he asked.

"I would've chosen Jonas over my job, yes. In retrospect."

"And me? Where do I fit in?"

"You will always be the father of my son."

"Is that all you think of me?" Logan wasn't sure whether to cry or take what she said as a joke.

"Until the day we can be transparent with each other, there will always be something between us, blocking us from truly being a couple," Marie said.

"So be transparent with me."

"I took an oath of office."

"Is the job more important than family? Than life?" Logan hoped he didn't go too far with this line of reasoning.

"No, but it's all I know to do."

"What is? Translating?"

"Serving my country."

"Which country? France? The USA?"

Marie didn't say.

"You didn't give up your US citizenship, did you?" Logan asked, suddenly alarmed.

"No. I was thinking about your question." Marie scooted out of her armchair and stepped away, as though Logan sitting there at her feet was too close for comfort.

Logan knew her well enough to know that it meant she couldn't handle talking further about it at this time. He decided he'd pray for her and try again another night. They had two more nights to go on the cruise.

Marie went to the small refrigerator. "Want some mineral water? Cranberry juice? Those are all I have."

"Water is fine." Logan peeled himself off the carpet and padded to the sliding glass door. "Look, it stopped raining. The moon is out. Let's go sit outside. We'll talk about our troubles later."

"Sounds good. I'll see you out there in a minute." Marie closed the bathroom door.

Logan stepped out onto the balcony, leaving the sliding glass door ajar behind him. The wind tossed his wavy hair a bit, and flapped his dress shirt. The rain had stopped.

A small dark cloud covered the moon. Logan looked up to see if it was going to rain again, and if the cloud would move. He wanted to get a photo of the moon.

The dark cloud was still there.

Oddly enough, the cloud started to come toward the small balcony, making weird motor or engine noises, and turning into odd-shaped shadows as they approached Logan—standing there with his jaw hanging down.

The cloud turned into what looked like several pairs of giant black boots—or something. Logan couldn't tell in the dim balcony light.

"What in the—"

Oomph!

The heavy objects made contact with Logan's

torso. He fell backwards, his shoulders smashing against the partially opened sliding glass door—

And he heard a sharp, loud crack in his left arm.

CHAPTER TWENTY-FIVE

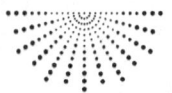

*M*arie stepped out of the bathroom to the sound of jetpacks and the sight of men in black landing on her small balcony. Someone in a light-colored shirt was moaning on the floor at the sliding glass door.

"Logan!" Marie ran toward her ex-husband, fully aware that her Sig Sauer was still locked inside the safe. Great. "Siri! Call security!"

The barrel ends of two handguns with silencers, each held by a different person, appeared in front of her nose.

"Make a move, Lucy, and your husband dies." His voice was gruff and slightly muffled behind the ski mask.

Marie wanted to correct him, but now wasn't the time. It was also pointless to try to pin down his accent. In today's world of mercenary work, he could be from anywhere.

Instead, she tried the benign. "Who is Lucy? You must have gotten the wrong stateroom."

"You both still die." Gruffy Voice nodded to the other intruder, who then slowly moved around Marie to point his gun at the back of her head.

God, help us.

Out there on the balcony, a fourth intruder was pulling Logan to his feet. He yowled in pain, holding his left arm. Marie couldn't tell if he had been shot.

Marie wasn't sure how she was going to defend herself and Logan against three armed men.

Well, she assumed they were men by their physiology, but Marie couldn't tell for sure since they all wore ski masks and hid behind Kevlar vests —or something similarly bulletproof—although it mattered not at this point. They had weapons. She had none.

There was little she could do standing in between the two men. She could do even less for Logan, now being hauled into the stateroom.

"Who are you?" Marie asked Gruffy.

No response.

"What do you want?"

Gruffy made a noise, something guttural, something unintelligible. To Marie, it sounded like a cross between a bear and an elephant.

"I guess you don't want money," Marie continued the charade.

She waited for more intruders to arrive, but these three were all there were.

"You know we're not in international waters." Logan grimaced.

"Oh, an intellectual." Gruffy muttered and expletive. To his men, he said, "Tie them up."

One of them went through his own pockets. "Uh..."

"You forgot the ties." Gruffy rolled his eyes.

The other intruder also did not have any cable ties with him.

Keystone Cops!

Thank You, Lord, for small victories before we all die.

Marie tried to contain her relief.

Gruffy pointed to the sofa. "Sit."

"You're in the USA." Logan sat down.

"Water is water. When we throw your dead bodies overboard, it doesn't matter who has jurisdiction. Dead is dead."

Gruffy turned to Marie. "Sit."

Marie did as she was told, but slowly. She prayed for wisdom. She reminded herself of her time in training and years in the field.

She glanced at Logan. He might not survive this.

I'm sorry, Logan.

"This is a cruise ship with over five thousand people," Logan said. "You can't hold all of us hostage."

Be quiet, Logan.

Marie tried to make eye contact with Logan, but he didn't look her way.

She could only pray that Siri on her iPhone in her purse on the side cabinet was smart enough to call shipboard security, not the one back at Ketchikan, which was probably too far away from them. Maybe Siri could call the Coast Guard.

She prayed that God would keep Jonas safer next door. Mrs. Ping shared the room to keep an eye on him. Marie guessed it was past midnight and they were both asleep.

Regardless, Mrs. Ping knew what to do in the event of danger.

Marie wished she could get a message to Mrs. Ping to get Jonas to safety. She could take him to the captain, and the shipboard security would know what to do about their hostage situation.

Speaking of whom, where was security?
Siri should have called them by now.

CHAPTER TWENTY-SIX

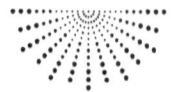

*T*his was not my idea of a family cruise.

Logan cradled his left arm against his ribs. He winced. He had quite a high tolerance for pain, but he knew he had to get medical help.

Lord, what is going on?

Who are these people?

Why do they think Marie's name is Lucy?

Logan counted three masked gunmen. There was no way he and Marie could fight their way out of this. First, they were unarmed. Second, Logan couldn't remember judo moves from middle school.

These days, he fought in corporate boardrooms and in online marketing battles.

Not on a cruise ship with people carrying silencers.

Yes, he knew what that was. Back in the days when the Urquhart family had armed bodyguards, Logan had learned a thing or two about weapons.

All this must have been a big mistake.

Could Marie be right? Could they have entered the wrong stateroom?

Or could this episode tonight be related to Marie's day job?

Logan was too afraid to move to reach out to Marie to hold her hand. She had her arms folded across her chest, her face revealing nothing. No fear. No worries.

That told Logan that she at least halfway knew what was going on here.

Who is Marie Bouchard, really?

Someday, she would have to come clean if she wanted their relationship restored. Then again, maybe it was best if they went their separate ways.

Why were these gunmen after her?

Clearly, they are not after me. I don't even have a parking ticket.

To be fair, Logan reminded himself that his full-time chauffeur drove him around.

The leader of the intruders made a phone call, speaking in a language that Logan didn't understand, but it sounded Middle Eastern. Maybe Arabic or Farsi or something else.

The man tapped his cell phone, and place it on the coffee table in front of Marie.

"Lucy." The voice on the phone was deep but calm.

There they go again, looking for Lucy.

Logan waited for Marie to respond. She didn't at first.

"I know you're there, Lucy."

Logan wondered why Marie didn't answer.

"You may not remember me, but Tel Aviv was mine."

"Failed work, Mr. Buchanan?" Marie asked.

"She speaks." Buchanan laughed.

What? What?

Logan felt a jab of pain in his broken elbow.

Tel Aviv? Logan was stunned. He had thought that Marie worked primarily in Europe. Was this a translation job? Logan had no idea that translators were in some sort of war.

Then again, Logan knew that Marie traveled wherever there was work. Still, Tel Aviv was a long way from France.

"If I hadn't trusted you..." Buchanan's voice trailed off.

"I'm only a translator," Marie said.

"So they all say."

"You know I'm telling you the truth."

"So says someone who used a fake name in my organization."

"I sometimes use an alias," Marie explained. Maybe more to Logan than for Buchanan's benefit.

"Your supervisor at the State Department or at the CIA made you do it?" Buchanan's voice grew deeper.

Logan's eyes widened. CIA. State Deparment.

He had no idea who he had married.

Marie didn't answer.

To Logan, it meant that Buchanan could be telling the truth, or Marie worked for neither, or she worked for one and not the other, or...

Logan felt a headache coming.

I'm a simple businessman, is all. I don't do spy games.

"No, Mr. Buchanan," Marie said. "Lucy is the name I would have named my daughter if I had one. It's a pretty name. You said so yourself."

Daughter? Logan felt uneasy. Had Marie been thinking of more kids? With whom?

"You chose to be Lucy in Yemen," Buchanan continued. "I know your real name, but I like Lucy better."

Yemen? Logan stared at Marie. Once again, she did not look at him.

"I was paid to translate." Marie's voice was even and calm. "I did my job, just as you did yours."

"You interrupted mine because you overheard something I said to my people. Then you disappeared for three years."

"I was assigned new projects. Like I said, I translate—"

Mr. Buchanan laughed. "I don't forget my enemies so easily, Lucy."

"Am I your enemy? I helped you avert a crisis in your organization, didn't I? Prevented you from taking a sabbatical in an Iranian prison when the missiles you sold to them turned out to be duds."

"Yes, you did—but you also spied on me for the USA and France and whoever else is involved."

"Like I said, Mr. Buchanan, I'm a translator. I translate when I am paid. I don't take sides."

"You don't have to take sides. You only have to pay back what I lost." Mr. Buchanan paused. "In fact, your husband and your son will pay on your behalf."

"You mean my ex-husband?" Marie asked. "We're currently not married to each other."

"From what we've seen the last few days, you might have gotten back together."

"What do you mean?" Logan finally spoke. "Have you been watching us?"

Was Buchanan implying that he had a spy onboard the cruise ship? Logan didn't know what to think except that his son could be in danger. He prayed that God would protect Jonas.

He regretted not hiring a bodyguard, but he had an aversion to them, after living most of his life under guard and scrutiny. *I am not as paranoid as Dad.*

"If I were you, Logan Urquhart, I wouldn't have let my wife go so easily," Buchanan said. "Then again, you're how we found her."

Before anyone could say another word, there came a knock on the door. "Room service!"

CHAPTER TWENTY-SEVEN

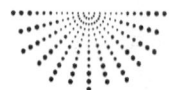

*G*ruffy ordered one of his men to usher Marie to the door. As they walked slowly, Marie spotted a small dagger in a sheath strapped to the man's left thigh.

With a pistol pressed against her spine, she answered the steward on the other side of the door.

"Your hot panini sandwich is ready, ma'am," came the reply. "Plus snacks for Mr. Urquhart."

Marie waited for Gruffy to tell her how to respond. When he didn't, she said, "Logan likes midnight munchies."

"You had dinner," Gruffy said.

"We're on vacation. I'll diet later," Marie said.

"Diet later? Or die now?" Gruffy grunted.

Behind him, the third gunman stood watch by

the closed balcony. The ceiling light reflected off the sliding glass door, such that one could not see outside. However, as the ship glided across the waters, Marie thought she saw movement outside, on her balcony.

She couldn't be sure.

She prayed that help had arrived.

"He'll be suspicious if we don't open the door." Marie stepped toward the closed door behind her, trying to keep Gruffy distracted and turned away from the balcony.

"He dies if he comes in—"

The noise of shattered glass interrupted Gruffy, as two figures in dark outfits burst through the broken balcony door, knocking down Gruffy's man at the door.

"Get down, Logan!" Marie yelled, as she tried to kick away the gun from her guard—but hesitated when she remembered she was barefoot.

It gave the gunman enough time to coil an arm around her neck and point the handgun at her temple.

Everyone froze.

Gruffy grunted. Both of his arms extended, a handgun in each hand, he addressed the new batch of intruders. "Well, who dies first?"

Marie's eyes darted toward Logan, who was on

the floor, sandwiched between the sofa and the coffee table. He didn't move.

Behind him, the two men who had entered the room were also wearing what looked like ski masks, exposing only their eyes—

Familiar eyes.

Zaid.

Marie couldn't believe it, but she tried to make eye contact with him. She wanted him to know that she could help—even if she didn't have shoes on.

Quietly she scolded herself for hesitating only moments earlier.

Help me get over it, Lord.

Having broken her big toe twice in her lifetime, Marie almost always wore closed-toe shoes—that was, when she was out and about. It hadn't crossed her mind to keep her shoes on inside the stateroom.

It also hadn't crossed her mind that Buchanan would track her down for three years and find her here in Alaska. How did he know about her personal alias?

That was one more thing she had to explain to Logan, who only ever called her Marie.

Somehow, Buchanan had also found out about her private life as Marie Bouchard.

And here we are.

Zaid was staring straight at her when Marie

looked in his direction. He seemed to be trying to tell her something.

She guessed that the man next to him must be one of Aliyah's bodyguards. The third one had to be still be with Aliyah.

Was Zaid there to help Marie and Logan? If he was, then he hadn't brought enough fighters.

"Now that we're all pointing our weapons at one another, please introduce yourself," Gruffy said to Zaid and his man.

Neither answered.

Zaid's eyes moved toward her bare feet.

I know. Marie sighed.

The gunman's grip on her neck and shoulder was strong.

Marie gasped. "Can't breathe."

She leaned back against the man, even though the barrel was still on her forehead. She tried to remember where the dagger was. Leaning against the man, she felt the sheath push against her left thigh.

There it is.

"Stand straight," he barked into her ears.

"Can't breathe." Her knees were wobbly.

"Marie!" Logan lifted his head above the coffee table. "Are you okay?"

Gruffy pointed one gun at Logan. "Sit down on the sofa!"

Logan got on his feet. His injured left elbow accidentally hit the edge of the coffee table, and he yelped.

Just then, the stateroom door behind Marie broke open.

Several armed security personnel poured in—

To gunfire.

CHAPTER TWENTY-EIGHT

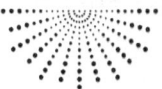

*H*owling like a wolf, Logan hoped to create enough distraction for their two rescuers to do something. What he didn't expect was to see Marie move so fast that in a split second, she had disarmed her guard, stabbed him—where did that dagger come from?—and knocked him unconscious to the floor.

She picked up his handgun.

Logan forgot about the pain in his elbow. All he could think of right now was that he had just seen his ex-wife make some moves unbecoming of a garden-variety translator.

All around her were dead people. The shipboard security was no match for the intruders.

Marie looked up, not at Logan, but at their two

other rescuers, the ones who had rappelled down to their balcony on ropes still hanging out there over the railing.

In front of Logan, with the tables and armchairs overturned, their rescuers were in close combat with the one intruder—the one who had spoken the most to Marie earlier.

Logan heard more engine noises coming from the sea. *Oh no.*

Two—three—more people landed on the balcony.

"Logan! Come on!" Marie yelled at him. "Now, Logan!"

Logan stumbled across the carpet toward Marie, but before he could reach her, Marie lunged forward and pinned him to the floor.

Logan heard gunfire. He closed his eyes.

He heard more gunfire, and then a thud.

He opened his eyes to see a man wearing night vision goggles sprawled out on the floor.

"Get up." Marie rolled off Logan, and pulled him out of the stateroom.

In the hallway, at least twenty feet away, more security personnel had assembled in the nook where they served snacks and morning buffet.

"Logan needs medical attention." Marie pointed to his left arm.

Someone nodded and radioed the ship's medical center.

"You're coming with me, right?" Logan asked.

"Soon. Zaid needs help." Marie surprised Logan with her answer.

"Zaid?" So their rescuers were Aliyah's bodyguards?

How did Marie recognize him behind his mask?

How well did Marie know Zaid?

A question for later.

Someone ran down the hallway toward them, his handguns by his side. It was Aliyah's third bodyguard.

Marie said something to him.

It sounded like Arabic.

Logan remembered that Marie had translated Arabic into French and English before. Which led him to wonder how much interaction Marie had with Zaid.

A small wrinkle of jealousy gripped Logan's heart.

Logan heard the name Omar, and guessed that it could be the bodyguard's name. He did not understand the rest of their back-and-forth in Arabic. The conversation ended when the bodyguard handed Marie two guns that somehow appeared out of his flak jacket.

Logan thought it was odd that the man trusted Marie with his weapons. Did he know who Marie was?

More than Logan knew?

Marie turned to one of the ship's security personnel who looked about the same size as she was. "Your vest, please."

Logan's heart beat faster. He didn't want her to die. "Marie?"

"Pray, Logan." And she followed Omar down the hall, back into her stateroom.

CHAPTER TWENTY-NINE

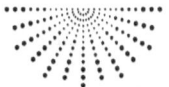

*B*y the time Marie and Omar returned to her stateroom, Zaid and his bodyguards had made a short work of the carnage. Gruffy was dead. So were his two accomplices and the second trio of assailants who had arrived via jetpacks.

Marie caught the end of the mess at the moment when Zaid kicked the handgun out of Gruffy's arm and stabbed his neck with a twisted blade.

When it came to close-contact combat, Marie had never seen anyone else better than the Zaid's men. She was impressed, and slightly scared at the same time. Her own Krav Maga training seemed like child's play compared to what Zaid had.

Maybe she could ask him to teach her how to disarm Buchanan's men that quickly. It was like Zaid had superhuman powers—either that, or Buchanan had sent rookies into the fight.

One last intruder raised his arms to get up from the floor, and Omar finished him before Marie could. She tried not to read too much into it, but Omar's smirk gave her the impression that he was delighted to be faster than she was.

Whatever. I'm not here to compete with you.

Marie had no idea how much time had lapsed. Covered in blood and sweat, she was exhausted as she stepped aside for the shipboard security to take over. Those bodies were no doubt going to the ship morgue.

The *Alaskan Queen of the Arctic Seas* was heading for the glaciers, and wouldn't be docking at a port until Friday. As far as the rest of the five thousand passengers were concerned, the cruise had been uneventful.

Even as six men lay dead in Marie's stateroom, spilling blood and guts all over the off-white carpet.

Marie wanted to get her things—her purse and the suitcase in her closet. Security debated whether she should, but she insisted that she needed her pajamas and her passport.

They sent a steward in with a trolley to get her

luggage, and told her they would take it to an empty stateroom, where she would stay for the rest of the cruise.

Her old stateroom was officially a crime scene.

In the hallway, it bothered Marie that Zaid had broken the necks of Buchanan's men. She would have rather kept them alive for INTERPOL interrogation.

"No need," Zaid explained in Arabic.

He seemed to wait for Marie to answer, as if testing her basic Arabic. He'd soon find out that she had already conversed with Omar in his mother tongue. Fluently.

"Because you've already traced Buchanan's point of origin while he was on the phone," Marie responded in English.

She knew it was a burner cell phone, and Buchanan was smart enough to use private VPNs. If INTERPOL, the FBI, the CIA, MI5, and MI6 could not find him the last three years, who was Zaid to succeed?

"If they were alive, you could ask them questions," Marie said.

"Is that what you do, generally? Play nice?" Zaid smirked. "These people killed millions with their weapons. We will track him down and take him home with us. He will be tried and executed for his crimes."

"So you know who was behind this." It was becoming clear to Marie now. "You were sending him a message by killing all six of his men."

"One was a woman."

"Oh, I didn't know. Then again, Buchanan is an equal opportunity arms dealer."

Zaid nodded. "When they boarded the ship, we thought they were pirates. But when Buchanan started talking, I contacted my office and found out that he is wanted in my homeland."

He spoke so casually that Marie wondered what kind of job Zaid did. "We who? Do you work for the captain?"

He laughed. "The captain works for us."

"Us who?"

"Her Royal Highness Aliyah's husband owns this cruise line."

"What?" Marie was surprised.

"You didn't google?"

"I was busy working."

"Of course." Zaid gave her a sly smile. "Please tell your boss at INTERPOL that Buchanan is ours."

He said INTERPOL.

Marie tried not to react. Zaid knew where she really worked.

"You don't have to worry. He won't be bothering you anymore."

Marie clammed up.

"We have just cause." A sly smile appeared on Zaid's face, ending at the scar on his cheek—which Marie hadn't been this close to notice. "His people sell weapons through my country and it's affecting our relationship with other countries, such as the United States. We now have an opportunity to end his activities."

"I'm just a simple translator." Marie didn't know why she felt that she had to say that. Her cover was blown now that Zaid knew she worked for INTERPOL. "I'm on vacation with my family, nothing more."

He ignored Marie. "It took a while to get to you. I'm sorry your husband was injured."

"Ex—never mind. You're not really a bodyguard for Aliyah, are you?"

"Her Royal Highness, you mean."

"I'm sorry. She introduced herself to me as Aliyah with no titles."

"We're trying to be low-key onboard. You better go clean up."

Marie nodded. "Thank you for rescuing Logan and me."

"We aim to keep our passengers safe. Next time you go on a cruise, do not hide under your real name."

Next time, I don't have to hide at all.

Marie lifted a finger. "One last thing."

Zaid frowned.

"What happened to Buchanan's phone on the coffee table?" Marie asked, anyway.

"What phone?"

CHAPTER THIRTY

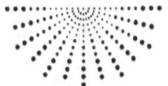

*I*n the medical facilities several decks below, the shipboard physician x-rayed Logan's arm and then paged a retired orthopedic surgeon who happened to be among the passengers on the cruise.

Between the doctors onboard the ship and their telemedicine associates at a partner hospital in Texas somewhere, they determined that Logan had a simple fracture in his left arm, near the elbow. It must've been where he had landed on the balcony when Buchanan's men invaded Marie's stateroom.

Watching the surgeon and the doctor put a cast on Logan's arm, Marie drew a sigh of relief. Her hair was still wet, but tied up in a ponytail. She had showered in her new stateroom, and changed into whatever clothes were still left in her suitcase that the steward had retrieved from her stateroom. It was a good thing that she had practically lived out of her suitcase. They had to bring her a new toothbrush and a tube of toothpaste, but she had everything else she needed for the rest of the cruise.

Except honesty between her and Logan.

Eventually they'd have to come clean with each other. However, if they never remarried, what would it matter? After what happened tonight, Logan might be done with her.

Just as well.

Some things were best left unsaid, unexplained.

By the time Marie accompanied Logan back to his own stateroom, it was nearly dawn.

"Come in for a minute?" Logan asked.

So he can interrogate me?

Marie couldn't decide if she should say yes or no. She had sent a secure message to both INTERPOL to advise them on what happened to her family. To be on the safe side, she also sent an encrypted message to her friend Esperanza, whose security firm had protected Jonas in the past. Maybe she could send the same person to accompany them home from Alaska.

"I know we're both tired, but I have some questions," Logan explained.

"I have many questions."

"But few answers."

With that statement, Logan confessed to Marie that he knew she wasn't going to be forthcoming with him.

She opened her mouth to say something.

"You don't have to come in. We're no longer married to each other, and we're not obligated to share the same space."

"Obligated?" Marie asked.

"Unless you want to come in and explain everything to me."

Marie took a deep breath. "I don't have all the details, to tell you the truth. But we can talk if it makes you feel better."

Logan held the door with his good arm.

Marie stepped inside the stateroom with the same configuration as hers—except without the gore.

Logan pointed to the sofa. "I'm going to change out of these clothes. Wait for me?"

He kicked off his blood-stained loafers, then tossed them into the trashcan. "I hope those bad guys didn't have diseases, because I got blood all over me."

"You better take a shower. I did."

"Did you throw away your clothes?"

"Yeah." Marie surveyed the room. The curtains were drawn, and it bothered her. She started walking toward them. "I didn't feel like getting them laundered."

"My thoughts exactly." Before he closed the bathroom door, he said, "Promise me you won't leave."

"I'll sit here and wait for you. Don't get your arm wet."

"I'll try not to."

The door closed, and Marie heard the shower head come to live.

She pulled the curtain open. Outside, a new day was dawning. Small streams flowed down the rocky mountains, streaked with rocks and snow. The ship glided across the water so slowly that small icebergs floating by looked like they were doing it in slow motion.

Every now and then a seal jumped up on an iceberg.

Jonas would have loved this.

Marie glanced at her watch. It was 5:21 a.m. He was probably still asleep.

Between cleaning up in her new stateroom and collecting Logan from the infirmary, she had stopped at Jonas's room to tell Mrs. Ping to be extra vigilant. There was no time to explain everything.

Mrs. Ping understood what was going on. In fact, Marie had told her more than what she had told Logan. Perhaps it was time for Logan to be in on the secret too.

"Ah, you're still here. Good."

Marie spun around. Logan was drying his hair with a towel. He was dressed in a pair of tee shirt and pajama pants.

"Let's sit and talk. Want some coffee? I'll ask the steward to bring some."

Marie shook her head. "I think you better lie down. I will bring a chair and sit with you."

"Yeah, the painkiller they gave me..." Logan offered to help Marie move a chair, but she said he could do it with more hands than he could spare.

Logan climbed into the bed on top of the bedspread, and waited for his ex-wife.

Ex-wife.

Sometimes Marie wondered how far they had fallen. How horribly they had treated their marriage vows before God. Even without an extra-marital affair, they had destroyed their relationship themselves.

"Who were those people who invaded your stateroom?" Logan asked.

"You heard the man on the phone." Marie sat

down in the armchair. It was lower than the bed. But it was very comfortable.

Logan got up and changed position. Lying sideways, his head was at the foot of the bed, his left arm on top of him.

"Buchanan. Who is he?" Logan asked.

Marie couldn't say.

"I heard what he wanted from you. Revenge or something. Talk to me, Marie."

Marie wondered how much she could tell for her story to be believable enough that Logan would stop asking more questions. How much could be declassified though?

"If I tell you anything, and Buchanan finds you, he will torture you to death for what you do not know," Marie said.

The way Logan looked at her, he seemed to believe her.

"If I put two and two together, I can say that some time ago, you translated for a man named Buchanan, but you heard too much. He tracked you down and found you here."

"Three years ago." Marie decided that it would be best if Logan led the discussion. Then she could tell him enough to satisfy his curiosity and keep him and Jonas safe.

"You were in Europe," Logan said.

"I flew back and forth to the Middle East. Part of the job."

"Was it around the time my PI found you?"

"I was back in Europe..." A sudden awareness washed over Marie. "Could that be how Buchanan found out my real name?"

Logan winced.

"I was under watch all the time when I worked on the project." Marie tried to sit straight up in her armchair, but her muscles ached. "Buchanan might have seen your PI interacting with me."

"Probably. Remember what Buchanan said?"

"Yes. You were how he found me."

"I'm sorry I got us into this mess." Logan rolled on his back.

"There's enough blame to go around." Marie quickly thought about her next step. "We need to find out whether your PI had interactions with anyone from Buchanan's organization."

"I could call him."

"No. I'll ask Espy. She'll send someone." She would probably send the same security personnel. "We don't want your PI freaking out."

Marie purposely did not mention INTERPOL. It would be too much for Logan to handle.

Then again, he had already heard Buchanan mention the CIA and the State Department.

Marie watched Logan lying upside down on the bed. "Don't fall asleep like that. I can't turn you back to put your head on the pillow."

"I'm just thinking about everything that happened tonight—how much we know and don't know."

The *don't know* part was what bothered Marie. There were many things she didn't know.

"Your ex-employer hating on you. Zaid coming to our rescue." Logan's eyes met Marie's. "Is there something you're not telling me?"

That was an impossible question.

If Logan had asked her if there was something she *needed* to tell him, then her answer was *no*.

Now she had to lie and lose her family—or what was left of it—all over again.

Or tell the truth and lose her job.

"I'm still looking for the truth myself," Marie said. "There are so many moving parts that I'm not completely certain what's going on."

"What are you saying?" Logan sat up at the edge of the bed. He looked serious, and maybe a tad unhappy.

"You need to get some sleep. Jonas will be up soon, and we need to take turns to watch him."

"Stop changing the subject, Marie."

"This is not a good time."

"When is?"

Marie didn't reply.

"There's never a good time for us, is there?" Logan asked. "We will always be keeping secrets from each other."

"Not always." Marie's voice was cracking now. "But for now... Until we get to the bottom of it..."

"You'll what?"

"I'll report what happened tonight to my boss. They need to take it from there." Marie got up from her armchair. She started to push it back to the sitting area.

"So there is nothing else you can tell me."

"Not much."

"That's why our marriage failed." Logan walked toward the door. "Your job is a giant black hole to me. I don't even know if you're really a translator. The way you took down the gunman... It was so fast, like a blur. Where did you get that dagger?"

"It was in a sheath on his thigh."

"How did you know it was there?"

"I've seen that kind before."

"At work?"

Marie nodded. "I see many things at work I can't talk about, Logan. Most of them are classified.

If I talk about them, people will die. We can't have that."

"Die? Do you work for the CIA?" Logan asked.

"Well, they do outsource translation to our company from time to time."

Marie didn't say that the CIA had actively tried to recruit her out of INTERPOL. Their reasoning was that she was an American citizen with French parents. They could use her help tracking down terrorists and working with multilingual informants. She turned them down because she didn't want to stay in Europe anymore.

"There're not the only ones who need translators. Every federal agency needs translators," she explained. "There are translators in the State Department and even at the United Nations."

"You used to do freelance translations," Logan reminded her.

"Those were the days. I can't go back now." *The country needs me.*

"In many ways, you're like soldier and I'm a civilian. Sometimes soldiers have to do things they can't talk about to civilians."

"Something like that, but I'm not a soldier. I'm only a translator, and when I work, they want me to keep my ears on the ground."

"Makes sense."

"I haven't told anyone else, but to tell you the truth, I don't want to do it anymore. I've missed three years of my son's life. He will be going to first grade soon. Am I going to miss the rest of his grade school?"

"I'm sorry."

"I'm glad you're there for him, but Mrs. Ping is only a substitute mother."

Logan was at the door, and Marie expected him to open it to let her out, but he didn't.

"You will always be Jonas's mother," Logan said softly. "That will never change."

"Birth mother in name only." Marie held back her tears.

CHAPTER THIRTY-ONE

*M*arie had never seen Logan this paranoid. If only he knew the awful truth of all the worst possible things that could have happened, he would have considered the events of the previous night not as bad.

However, Marie couldn't tell him. She wished she could, but there was no way to breach security protocols without letting him in on what she had to deal with at the time of their separation and divorce three years before.

Jonas was still bawling, thumping his arms on his bed. "Wanna see geezers! Daddy, please?"

"I don't want to lose you." Logan looked at Jonas first, then at Marie.

Marie wasn't sure what he was implying. Surely the little incident in Ketchikan couldn't have affected Logan this badly. Had something happened back in Atlanta that Marie didn't know about?

"You can see the glaciers from the lounge." Logan tried to put shoes on Jonas with one hand, but the boy was kicking. "It's on the top deck with windows all around."

"No-no-no-no!" The poor brat protested. "Wanna be outside!"

"It's cold outside."

"I have a jacket, Dad! You made me bring it, remember?"

Marie glanced at Mrs. Ping, who busied herself opening and closing drawers, and wiping the same tabletops multiple times.

Marie looked inside her purse. She didn't want to do this, but maybe an RFID brooch on Jonas might help—

No.

They were still on a ship. How far could Jonas go? Into the water? If Jonas was in any kind of danger, it wouldn't be from an abduction.

Jonas screamed.

"Aargh." *I can't think.*

Marie took Jonas's shoes from Logan's hands, and motioned for Logan to step aside. It was her turn to deal with their son.

Lord, You made this child. You created him in my womb. Help me deal with him according to Your perfect will.

Marie sat down next to Jonas on the edge of the bed. "Jonas."

Jonas sat up. "Yes, Mommy?"

"Do you know why glaciers are blue?"

Jonas shook his head.

"Do you know that light has seven colors?"

"No."

"Do you know that blue light has short wavelengths?"

"What?"

"Exactly. Now all that information is important if you want to know more about glaciers." Marie dug inside her purse and produced a small notebook with a pen attached to it. "Do you know what this is?"

"Paper."

"And pen." Marie held the notebook gently in her hand, as if it were the most fragile thing in the world. "Are you a big boy, Jonas?"

"Yes, ma'am!"

"I'm going to give you this notebook and the

pen—it's not a pencil—and I need you to take notes when the geologist tells you anything new about glaciers."

"What is a joe gist?"

"A geologist is someone who studies rocks."

"Wow. People study rocks? I just throw them and see if they smash!" Jonas eyed the notebook. "Is that a real pen? Daddy won't let me touch a pen."

"Because he opens it all up and spills the ink on the carpet," Logan said from where he was sitting.

"I can only use pencils." Jonas curled his lips.

"Well, today is a special day," Marie said. "If you promise to give this notebook back to me with new information about glaciers, I will let you use my pen for the day."

"I can't write, Mommy."

Marie glanced at Logan. "He's five. I wrote when I was three!"

Logan shrugged. "He's normal. You're not."

"I don't know about that. Does he know his alphabet?" Marie felt a tug on her sleeve.

Two eyes filled with tears looked up at her. "Will you teach me to write with that pen, Mommy?"

Marie hugged her son. "Of course. We will start today."

"Today?"

Marie nodded. She handed the notebook and pen to Jonas. "Do you have a pocket?"

Jonas pointed to the pockets on his pants.

"Too small. We can put it in your backpack then." Marie waved to Mrs. Ping to bring her his backpack.

Mrs. Ping emptied out the crayons and toys from Jonas's backpack.

"You might want to put the crayons and drawing pads back into the backpack," Marie told her. "Jonas might want to draw glaciers."

Jonas's eyes brightened. "Yes! I love to draw."

Marie handed Jonas his shoes. "You're a big boy and you can put on shoes yourself, right?"

"Yes. I also know left and right." Jonas set out to prove to his mom that he could press the Velcro over his shoes too.

Velcro. The invention for all ages.

"Well, good. We need to go now if we want to see the glaciers." Marie put her notebook and pen into Jonas's backpack, next to the drawing pad and crayons.

"You're going to need your jacket," Marie said.

Logan let out a giant sigh.

"We're going outside?" Jonas asked.

"We are all going to put on our jackets, but your

job is to take notes with my pen," Marie said. "In order to take notes, you're going to need to sit at a table so that you can have nice handwriting."

Jonas nodded. "I hope they have tables outside."

Marie smiled. "We will find a table, where we can still hear the geologist when he explains this and that."

"So that I can write down this and that."

"Exactly."

Mrs. Ping held Jonas's hand as they walked toward the door. A worried look was on her face. "Where to?"

"We'll go together. Take the elevator up to the top deck." Marie zipped up her own jacket.

She was following Mrs. Ping out of the stateroom when she felt someone grab her arm. Before she could ask Logan what he wanted, he answered her question without a word.

As soon as their lips met, Marie could see their wedding day on Cumberland Island once again, barefoot in the sand, surrounded by wild horses and old ruins. She could see the way Logan had stared at her in her simple wedding gown, with only a sheer veil separating him from claiming her lips.

She could hear the preacher pronounce them

husband and wife. The cheers of their family. Their happy reception at the historic home across the water in the small town of St. Mary's. Their excited dash to the private plane that flew them to England for their honeymoon.

Three years later, they were divorced.

CHAPTER THIRTY-TWO

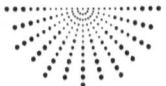

"If you stay close to Mommy and Daddy, like holding our hands all the time, we can be safe. Okay?" Marie said to Jonas.

Her voice sounded so serious, like it was the most important thing in all the world.

Logan wasn't sure what to do at this point. He had specifically told Jonas they were not going outside. And here they were, in the elevator, going to the top deck.

He glanced at Marie, but could not read what was on her mind. To be honest, all he could think of were her warm lips—

He cleared his throat.

To be fair to Marie, he had no idea if she was

going to lead them outside. Also, the top deck was there the lounge was.

On the one hand, Logan could insist that he was the head of this household, and that Marie—who did not have custody of their son—should not have overridden his instructions to his own son. It made him look bad in front of both Jonas and Mrs. Ping. The latter might think that Marie had undermined his authority.

"Daddy, you better hold my hand." Jonas reached for Logan's right hand. "We don't want you to fall over since you only have one arm left."

Logan chuckled. Thanks to the painkillers, his broken elbow-in-a-cast didn't hurt.

He almost forgot what he was thinking.

Logan wished he knew more about what was going on in Marie's life—whether her job would continue to endanger all of them. He wanted her to quit. He earned enough to support all three of them for the rest of their lives. They didn't need Marie's salary.

He whispered in Marie's ear, "I need to talk to you tonight about something."

As if misreading him, Marie said something else. "This is the only time we get to see the glaciers up close. Tomorrow we'll be in Victoria, then Seattle, then home."

I get it. Still...

The elevator door opened.

People were walking back and forth, some carrying binoculars. There were multiple doors leading here and there—at least two going outside and two more leading to the lounge where Logan had originally planned to take Jonas.

Above their heads, the intercom broadcast something. "To your left, you can see seals jumping onto small icebergs. If you look through your binoculars, you might be able to see mountain goats climbing up and down the side of the mountains."

Marie stepped to one side of the hallway. She knelt down so that she could be at eye level with Jonas.

"We're going to send Dad outside to check the wind and weather, okay?" Marie said. "We don't want to get sick if it's too cold outside."

Jonas nodded.

"So we're going to wait in the lounge. There's a door we can send Dad out. You can help me close the door, and then we have to open it again to let Dad in."

Jonas rolled his eyes.

"What?" Marie asked.

"You're making a very big deal out of this, Mommy."

"I am? Safety first."

"Are we going outside or not?" Jonas's voice was breaking up.

"We will make a decision based on the information that Daddy is going to gather for us."

Jonas looked puzzled.

Oh dear. Logan squatted down. "Like Mommy said, safety first. Would you prefer I check outside or shall we send Mrs. Ping?"

"Send Mrs. Ping. She's nice to me."

Mrs. Ping laughed. "I don't spoil him ever."

"I'll go if you wait in there." Marie pointed to the lounge. "Find a table, Jonas. Save me a seat. Can you order hot chocolate for me?"

"They have hot chocolate?" Jonas asked.

"Inside." Logan wasn't sure if it was true or not. He was also sure they could take their cups outside. But whatever.

"If the coast is clear, we'll go outside now and drink hot chocolate later," Marie said.

Reverse psychology or what? Logan tried to keep a straight face.

"I want hot chocolate now."Jonas tugged at Logan's good arm. "Let's go, Daddy."

Ice cream and hot chocolate.

That's all Jonas needs.

CHAPTER THIRTY-THREE

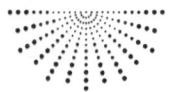

The first person Marie saw outside on the deck was Zaid. She looked around to see if Aliyah's entourage were there, but no. She wondered if Abdul would have liked to see the glaciers too.

The ship was cruising very slowly. The sunny day made everything look bright. A chilly breeze swept across the deck, and made her nose feel cold, but otherwise Marie liked the weather.

She could hear echoes of glaciers breaking off in the distance.

"In a few minutes, we will reach our first glacier," the geologist said through the intercom.

Enough time for Marie to go back inside and get Jonas.

The deck was not as crowded as Marie had expected. She was able to look past the crowd, toward the distance, where two cruise ships were making their way back. Those ships were probably why this ship had to wait its turn until this afternoon.

Zaid must have spotted her. He came her way.

"Good afternoon." He did not use her name.

Marie returned the greeting. She switched to Arabic. "Is everything okay?"

"Very safe, ma'am." Zaid seemed pleased that Marie chose to speak to him in his mother tongue. "Where is your family?"

"Hiding in the lounge until I tell them that the coast is clear." Marie looked that way only to see Jonas's face plastered to the window.

Zaid grinned. "The coast is clear. Look around and be assured."

So Marie did.

And was surprised to see men with earbuds and wearing thick jackets spread all over the deck, trying to look normal and trying to blend in. They were from all nationalities, it seemed. Had they been onboard the ship all this time?

"They arrived this morning," Zaid said quietly, as if sensing her question.

"Did you get any sleep?" Marie regretted asking. She did not want Zaid to think she was showing any interest in him.

"Did you and Logan get any sleep?"

"Barely."

"Same."

"Why can't we have a nice family vacation?" Marie asked, knowing the answer was never simple in a complicated world.

"Because of evil people."

"Bad."

"No. Evil. Absolutely evil." Zaid stepped away. "You have a nice day."

Marie walked toward the door that led to the lounge. It had three doors. Two on the inside, and this one on the outside. She waved to Jonas at the window. He waved back.

The kid had no idea how complex life was. All Marie could do was try her best to make their environment as safe as possible for Jonas and the next generations to grow up in.

Sometimes it felt like a losing battle.

But then God is always victorious.

Praise the Lord.

"Mommy, look who's inside too?" Jonas pointed to Abdul at the next table.

Sitting next to Jonas, Logan pointed to an empty spot on the upholstered bench that went all around the bottom of the windows.

"Thanks for saving me a seat. Where's Mrs. Ping?" Marie sat down.

Logan pushed a mug of hot chocolate toward her on the small table in front of them. "She's gone to check if we could meet the geologist."

On the other side of Logan, Jonas was showing Abdul his new notebook. "This is Mommy's pen. Want to see how it works?"

Abdul nodded. Jonas began to scribble in the notebook. "I'm taking notes about the geezers."

Several people turned their heads toward Jonas.

"Glaciers," Logan explained. "We're still working on pronunciation and everything else."

A few of the elderly passengers nodded.

"It's safe outside," Marie said quietly to Logan, just in case Jonas had altogether forgotten about the glaciers.

"As of two minutes ago?" Logan whispered.

"Trust God to keep us safe." Marie swiped her phone, tapped a few times, and showed Logan what she had screen captured and saved. It was Psalm 61:3, one of her favorite verses that God had brought to her mind many times over while she had been behind enemy lines.

For You have been a shelter
for me,
A strong tower from the
enemy.

"I like that. Email it to me?" Logan asked.

"Sure." And she did.

Logan's right hand reached for her left hand. Marie didn't protest.

~

"Whoa!" Jonas jumped up and down on the deck as another giant chunk of glacier crashed into the cold sea.

He urged Abdul to jump too. Abdul glanced at his mother, as if looking for permission. She smiled and nodded slightly.

The two boys jumped and shouted, "Whoa!"

Surrounding them were the two families, although Abdul's family seemed to have more bodyguards today than in Ketchikan. Speaking of which, Logan had changed his mind about that morning only the day before. He was confident now that Jonas had been safe walking about with Abdul's family.

His concerns had been unfounded.

Logan wasn't sure who among the crowd were part of Abdul's protection unit, and he wished that he were more observant. He decided to ask Marie later—if he had a chance—whether she noticed new people in the crowd.

Marie was standing next to Abdul's mother and her assistant. None of them said a word to one another. They stood there, smiling. Marie was taking photos of Jonas, the glaciers, and then back to Jonas.

Logan lost track of what the geologist was talking about. It looked like Jonas had also forgotten that he had been assigned to take notes. The backpack carrying all that school stuff was now in Marie's hands.

Somehow Logan felt a bit safer in the crowd. Like nobody in their right minds would try to take down a thousand people milling about on this open deck.

Besides, Marie had informed him that the ship had beefed up security after what happened on Wednesday night. The evidence had to be all around them, although Logan couldn't tell with everyone wearing thick jackets in the chilly weather. Yeah, it was still July, but there was ice all around them.

Logan made eye contact with one of Zaid's men whom he recognized. He was sure they all knew who he was—a civilian who had survived some sort of terrorist attack in Marie's stateroom, and had war wounds to prove he had been there in person.

CHAPTER THIRTY-FOUR

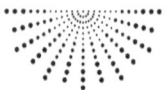

"Yes, I believe that's the safest thing to do, considering all that we went through," Marie said to Logan after dinner when they had time alone.

Logan seemed to have expected their evening walk on the deck, and she didn't want to disappoint him. The night was cloudy, and the air nippy, but they walked anyway.

It was their last night on the cruise.

"When we tell Jonas in the morning, I don't know how he'll react," Logan asked quietly. He didn't hold her hands, but he was walking close enough to put his good arm around her shoulder, although he did not.

"Safety first. If he doesn't understand now, he will understand later."

"Interestingly, his friend is staying through until the ship docks in Seattle on Saturday."

"That's their choice." Marie wasn't entirely certain that beefing up security was enough to protect anyone. However, Zaid seemed to think it was plenty, especially since they suspected that their boy was not in any danger.

In fact, Zaid had made it clear to her that she had brought danger to the cruise.

"I shouldn't have come," Marie said.

"You had no idea it wasn't completely over." Logan didn't say more, but he seemed to indicate that he could put two and two together.

"Now we know it isn't." Marie was still waiting for a reply from Mendenhall Security. As soon as she could, she had sent an encrypted message to Esperanza.

She had also contacted her INTERPOL office in France, who had connected her to the INTERPOL National Central Bureau in Ottawa.

Everyone had been informed.

But Esperanza's concerns made Marie worry. To her credit, the security specialist did not trust anyone else to go after Buchanan. She wanted to do it herself.

Marie had thought Esperanza would be satisfied that Molyneux was finally behind bars, but apparently not. As long as the terrorist was still alive, her associates thought they could roam free and rule the world.

Buchanan seemed to be one such prideful creature.

"We can always return to Victoria," Logan said.

Marie nodded. "Of course. It's only a flight away."

"Sometimes a child needs to know that we parents do things for their safety."

"And they may not understand it at first—much like how we might pitch a fit at God whenever He tries to keep us safe."

Logan stopped walking. "Did you just say *pitch a fit*? Going southern belle on me?"

Marie ignored his small talk. "We need to talk to Mrs. Ping about tomorrow."

"Why? Isn't she coming home with us?"

"Technically you paid for the entire trip. If I go home with you until Sunday, there's no reason she can't stay for the rest of the trip and enjoy what little cruise is left."

"We're assuming she's in no danger."

"She can protect herself."

Logan raised his eyebrows. "Something else you're not telling me?"

"She has a black belt in martial arts, as we know," Marie said, not giving anything else away. Like the five one-week weapons training that Esperanza had given Mrs. Ping, who had been in the police force—albeit a desk job—in Hong Kong before her family emigrated to the USA twenty years ago. She was rusty in the weapons department, but Esperanza polished off the grime.

"Maybe she should be with us, then, to help us keep Jonas safe."

"Espy is sending someone to your house as we speak. We'll be fine."

"We will?" Logan smiled. "I can't believe you'll be spending a couple of days at home."

"Your home."

"It's also yours. It will always be yours—if you want."

Marie didn't want to go there. "The most important thing right now is to make sure Jonas is safe."

"Our safety is in God's hands. Remember the verse you gave me yesterday?" Logan swiped his phone. "Let me read the email back to you. 'For You have been a shelter for me, a strong tower from the enemy.' Psalm 61:3."

"Amen." Marie turned around.

They were only halfway down the top deck. Marie felt an urgent need to return to Jonas's stateroom. She didn't have to, but she felt like she needed to watch her son sleep, as if time was running out.

"Are we going back already?" Logan asked.

"I think I'll turn in early tonight. By now Mrs. Ping would have gotten Jonas ready for bed."

On the way down the stairs, Logan said he was glad Marie came on the cruise.

"Or you wouldn't hear the end of it from Jonas." Marie laughed.

"That too. But more than that, I am glad you're here. I think this was the best week of our marriage —barring a few things—don't you think?"

Marie stepped off the stairs onto the wood floor next to a sliding glass door that faced a railing and the ocean beyond. Logan tugged at her hand, and pulled her toward him, ever so gently, as if he would be okay with it if she declined his invitation.

She was curious. Where was he going with this?

"I just want—need—a hug," Logan confessed.

I can hug. And so she did.

They held each other in the small balcony,

night wind in their hair, the slushing noise of the waves disappearing into Marie's thoughts of long lost-homes and missed affections.

Of a little boy who wanted his mother.

Of an ex-husband who still cared.

"I will always love you," he whispered.

Was that the wind in her hair speaking what she wanted to hear?

"I've mistaken you five ways through Christmas, but I want to make amends now." Logan kept his voice low. For her ears only.

"What does that even mean—five ways through Christmas?"

"I don't know."

"Then why say it?" Marie chuckled.

"Because it sounds good."

"Christmas sounds good?" Marie remembered the first two years they had been married, the lovely Christmases they had—and the overkill they did to please their small child.

"I want you home for Christmas—if it's at all possible," Logan said.

"I can check my schedule to see." The night was darkening, and even with the small lamp by the door, Marie could not read Logan's eyes or his deep thoughts.

"That will be great if you can. If there's even a remote possibility..."

"Maybe."

"Maybe? I'll take *maybe*. It's better than *no*."

Yes, it's better than no.

CHAPTER THIRTY-FIVE

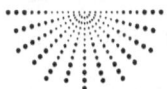

The next morning, Logan had second thoughts about their plans when they docked at the Victoria Cruise Ship Terminal at Ogden Point on the south end of Vancouver Island, Canada. He had packed his one suitcase, and was making a final walk around his stateroom to make sure he hadn't left anything behind—like his power cord or his credit card.

Outside on the balcony, the Friday morning air was crisp and the sky was clear, yet the atmosphere held a foreboding of the one event that Logan had been trying not to think about for several days now: separation.

Before the cruise, he dreaded the whole affair. His marriage with Marie hadn't worked out, so why would he want to relive it? Even though it was only for seven days, he had the idea that they'd both be miserable, putting on false smiles for their son's sake.

Now, at the end of their week together, Logan wondered if he had misjudged Marie while they had been married. Although she hadn't totally come clean about her job—or jobs—he sensed that she would eventually do so when she was ready.

Am I ready to hear what she has to say?

"I should focus on the positives of our relationship," Logan said to no one.

This week, they had touched each other, even kissed, more than they ever did in three years. For that, Logan knew he had to be grateful.

Hours from now, they would go their separate ways. She would go back to France to resume whatever job she said she did. Logan would remain in Atlanta, without the woman he loved.

Loved?

Yes, loved.

Logan didn't want to recall how his anger had caused him to distance himself from Marie, to hate on her. Perhaps he had been jealous that her job was so important to her that she couldn't tell him anything about it, leaving him wondering. Perhaps being a translator was all she really did, and he had read too much into her life, assumed too much, imagined too much.

Logan shook his head. "You want me to believe that you're just a garden variety translator? Not after that night."

It was still a blur in his mind. In the comfort of his own home next week, Logan would try to process what went on that night, when they were both nearly killed.

Maybe it was best if he and Marie never got back together again after this.

On the other hand, Logan knew that they both still had feelings for each other. Whether they were new feelings or revived from their dating days and the honeymoon year of their marriage, he could not be sure. But he knew that, if he could have a second chance with Marie, he would take it.

I want her back.

But does she want to come back to me?

Logan picked up a sock from the closet floor and stuffed it into his suitcase. He decided he would launder everything when he got home to Atlanta. He wasn't like Marie, who had separate compartments in her suitcase so that her dirty clothes did not mix with her clean clothes. Sometimes she even used a large trash bag to put her dirty clothes in before she packed her suitcase to go home from their vacations. And she would never throw her shoes on top of the clothes. Shoes went into their own bags.

Is she still like that today or has she changed some?

Logan zipped up the suitcase and rolled it to the door. He debated whether to make another sweep of the stateroom—like Marie would.

He almost did, but his phone rang.

It was Mrs. Ping. Her voice sounded unsure and excited at the same time, and Logan prayed that she wouldn't throw a curveball at him.

Logan took a deep breath and listened.

Ah, Mrs. Ping wanted to go see the flowers at Butchart Gardens. She said she would be safe with the captain.

"Did I hear that correctly?" Logan wasn't sure his ears were working right. "Did you say the captain? As in the captain of this ship?"

"My companion for the day. He's widowed, as I am."

"Is he? How did you know that?"

"We've talked."

"Talked?" Logan almost asked her when she had the time to talk with the captain, and then he remembered all the times he and Marie had taken

Jonas off Mrs. Ping's hands and given her a lot of time off.

So that's what she's been doing with all that extra time. Chatting with the captain.

"He's seen me around. We eat dinner at the same time as he does, remember?" Mrs. Ping said.

"We do? I don't recall."

"Yes, whenever we come and go from the dining hall, I see him walking about. I thanked him for doing such a great job, and he offered to give me a personal tour of this beautiful ship."

"A personal tour?" *This is getting serious.*

"Anyway, he introduced us to the geologist—remember we did that yesterday? The next thing I knew, he offered to show me around Butchart Gardens."

They have official tour guides there, you know.

"He contacted you." Logan made the statement, knowing that Mrs. Ping was lost to her newfound beau. How was that going to affect their plans for the day?

"He sent me this pretty card—the steward brought it to me not half an hour ago—and offered to spend the day with me."

"Wow."

"I know, right? Wow."

Logan took a deep breath. He needed Mrs.

Ping to be with Jonas. They were leaving Victoria—and the cruise ship—for Atlanta.

"Our flight is at noon," Logan reminded her. Of course, she knew that.

"That's why I called."

Logan heard a knock on the door.

"Wait a second," Logan said. "Someone's at the door."

"It's me."

"You didn't have to call if you're standing outside." Logan sighed. He unlocked the door.

There was Mrs. Ping, blushing and grinning and all.

"Are you blushing?" *She's in love.*

She cleared her throat. "If it's okay with you Mr. Logan, I would like to stay on the ship for the rest of the cruise. We dock in Seattle tomorrow, anyway, and you've already paid for my plane ticket back to Atlanta. I will be there by Saturday night, as was in our original cruise plan. Marie said she will stay until Sunday after church before she flies home to France."

Logan's heart nearly skipped a beat. "She said that?"

Mrs. Ping nodded. "I talked to her before calling you."

"What else did she say?"

"She said she will only do this if you agree."

"Of course." *I want her to stay with me past Sunday!*

"Good. She wasn't sure if you will go for it."

"No? Did she say why?"

"Because she wants us to stay together and fly home together today. She doesn't want to disrupt Jonas's routine or your plans."

"Plans?" *My plan is for her to stay with me for the rest of our lives.*

The captain's voice came over the public address system, and Mrs. Ping blushed again.

"Ladies and gentlemen, we've arrived in Victoria, British Columbia. Please make sure to have your passport and boarding pass with you before you disembark for your excursions and activities. No need to bring umbrellas today because it will be a beautiful and sunny day on the island. Have fun, everyone!"

"All right, Mrs. Ping," Logan said. "We will see you in Atlanta on Saturday night. Text Wallace to make sure he picks you up at the airport."

Mrs. Ping's face looked concerned. "Will you be fine with Marie, Mr. Logan?"

"What do you mean?"

"Are you getting along?"

"We get along, surprisingly." Logan chuckled.

"If you're implying you're worried that we might fight on the flight home to Atlanta, you can put that to rest. We haven't fought all week."

"Maybe the fresh Alaskan air helped."

"God helped."

"Yes, for sure. I have been praying for you two."

"Thank you, Mrs. Ping." He didn't want to talk more. "We better go. Is Jonas still in your room?"

"No. Marie took her downstairs. They're probably waiting near the gangplank."

"Wow. So we know all the different parts of the cruise ship now, don't we?"

Mrs. Ping smiled. "I'm a fast learner."

CHAPTER THIRTY-SIX

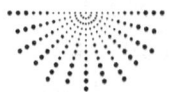

*M*arie didn't know how to stop Jonas from sobbing into her blouse. It was all wet on one side, near her hip. He seemed to try his best to keep his crying quiet because there were other kids around. The crowd in the foyer was noisy, and nobody seemed to pay any attention to a weepy five-year-old.

There was so much of Logan in Jonas.

All Marie could do was pray for Jonas that God would surround him with His protection for the rest of his life. She might not be around until the time when Jonas was old, but eternal God would always be there for him.

And for Logan too.

She prayed silently that Jonas would someday

believe in Jesus Christ, the strong tower whom Jonas could run to whenever he needed shelter from the storms in life. She knew the storms would come, but she prayed that Jonas would be ready for them.

God would shelter him.

Marie had no doubt about it. She recalled the verse she had shared with Logan on the morning the ship arrived at the glacier fields. Psalm 61:3 had been her anchor verse in the last three years of her career.

For You have been a shelter
for me,
A strong tower from the
enemy.

She wanted to retire sooner than later—before the job killed her. Marie wondered if she could call it quits by Christmas so that she could spend the season at home—

Home?

Home as in Logan's house?

Well, she could always rent a condo nearby, in Buckhead somewhere, so that Jonas didn't have to go too far to see her. Maybe they could rework their custody agreement so that she could get equal time with her son.

And what about Logan?

Marie didn't know what to think about Logan. He had taken it like a man that night when Buchanan's men broke into her stateroom.

She thanked God that Logan wasn't hurt beyond the broken arm.

It could have been so much worse.

In fact, Buchanan could have come for Jonas.

Marie was sure that as long as Buchanan was still alive, he would. He probably had Logan's Atlanta house staked out by now.

Marie would be eternally grateful to her friend Esperanza who had pretty much put herself in charge of her family's safety.

Marie had received a message from Esperanza the night before, stating that her security company would ensure the safety of Logan and Jonas if Marie helped Mendenhall Security to track down Buchanan.

It sounded like Esperanza did not want Zaid to get to Buchanan first. However, she did not tell Marie why. Marie could guess that what Buchanan knew about his terrorist associates would be more valuable to Esperanza than his head on a platter in Zaid's execution court.

"I want a free shirt and a woolly mama!" Jonas whined as he pushed away from Marie.

"You can get a free shirt anywhere." Logan rolled his suitcase to a stop next to Jonas's suitcase. "Did you mean a specialty tee shirt?"

"*Especially* tee shirt." Jonas sniffled. His eyes were like puppy dog eyes.

Marie debated whether to tell him to stop that nonsense or to let Logan handle it. She chose the latter.

"And a woolly mama!" Jonas raised his hands up in the air.

"Mammoth," Logan corrected him.

"What I said, Daddy. Woolly mama!"

Tall order, Marie supposed.

Instead of answering Jonas, Logan turned to Marie. "How are you this morning?"

"I'm fine. How's your arm?" Marie asked.

"All my x-rays have been sent to my physician in Atlanta. I'll be seeing an orthopedic specialist on Monday."

"Good." She waited to see if Logan was going to talk to Jonas.

He did not.

Jonas detached himself from his mother's side, strutting in a circle, making elephant noises. He was in his own little world now.

"He needs siblings to play with," Marie blurted before she realized she had spoken aloud.

Logan's eyes were on her. "I hope not half-siblings."

Before Marie could respond, she heard Jonas call out, "Abdul!"

"Abdul!" He waved to an entourage coming down the stairs. "Mommy, can I go talk to him?"

"Wait until they get here. This is where we assemble to get off the ship," Marie said, waving her hand around her in the foyer. However, most of the people were in the lounges, waiting for their sections to be called. The Urquharts had drawn an A, and would be the first ones off the ship.

"What *sample*?" Jonas asked.

"Assemble. Stay here. He's coming this way." Marie waved to Aliyah, who waved back—slightly.

The princess looked a bit sickly, and her hand was on her stomach.

Uh oh. Marie wondered if it was something she ate. She had heard of passengers getting food poisoning onboard cruise ships. However, she had been well this entire trip, and hadn't heard of anyone else getting sick. That didn't mean there weren't actual cases of people getting sick while on a cruise—or vacation, for that matter.

Aliyah's palm went to her face and she dashed

around the corner in the direction of the ladies' restroom. Her assistant spat out orders to the men around Abdul—including Zaid and Omar—before she ran after Aliyah.

"If it's time to go, wait in the vehicle for us. Leave Omar here to escort us down." Or something like that. Marie had only heard parts of it because the assistant spoke quickly, and the foyer was crowded with people talking and laughing.

Abdul pointed to Jonas. Jonas was still making elephant noises. Next thing Marie knew, the two boys were walking like elephants—or Woolly Mamas.

Zaid barely nodded to Marie and Logan. He didn't say anything to them even though he was only a few feet away from them. His eyes looked tired.

Not a morning person?

Marie's watch said it was quite early still, even though the sun was rising. If their circumstances hadn't changed, they'd all be looking forward to a fun day in Victoria. She hadn't been to the gardens in years, and would love to join Mrs. Ping on the tour—even though she might end up being the third wheel.

She wondered what Logan would have liked to do in Victoria. He was the type who might enjoy the natural history museum. Well, Marie would too. It would have been a happy family vacation.

"Sorry we're going to miss Victoria," Marie said to Zaid.

"You're sorry?" Zaid raised an eyebrow. "Thank God you're alive."

"I thank God every day," Marie said.

"Good."

Aliyah returned, and their group went to the front. Marie assumed the princess didn't need to draw a number and wait their turn.

Jonas seemed sad to see his friend go. Marie thought that maybe later in the year or sometime, she could call the number on Zaid's business card and invite them over.

You know, just like that.

Marie chuckled at her own naïveté. Surely a prince wouldn't be that easy to invite.

Logan leaned toward her ear. "Something funny?"

Marie didn't get to answer. She pointed to the people coming out of an elevator.

Mrs. Ping and the captain of the *Alaskan Queen of the Arctic Seas.*

She was wearing a wide-brimmed hat that matched her bright lime green blouse. Marie didn't remember her wearing anything bright in the last five years. She might have gone shopping in Ketchikan or onboard the ship.

And what is that? Lipstick? When was the last time Mrs. Ping had worn lipstick?

Marie was smiling and thinking all those thoughts, and didn't realize Logan was holding her hand.

It was obvious that she had indeed let her guard down with Logan to the point that she wasn't bothered that his fingers were entwined in hers.

He squeezed her hand gently.

It still didn't bother her.

Is this good or bad?

CHAPTER THIRTY-SEVEN

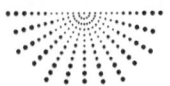

*L*ogan wondered what went through Marie's mind as they walked across the gangplank ahead of a porter rolling a luggage cart containing their three suitcases. Jonas had insisted on carrying his own backpack, so he did.

Marie was looking in the direction of the parking lot, where the royal family was climbing into two SUVs with tinted windows.

Aliyah and Abdul went in the first vehicle. The assistant and one of the bodyguards went into the second one. Zaid and another bodyguard were talking to each other outside the vehicles.

"Where's our ride?" Logan asked.

Marie pointed to a black SUV that was making

its way around a row of tour buses—some were double-decker buses painted red—toward them. "We have enough time to get to the airport."

"Forty minutes. When's our flight?"

"Any time we're ready."

"Ah, yes. I forget." A private plane courtesy of Mendenhall Security.

If they had flown commercial, it would take them at least nine or ten hours to get to Atlanta from the Victoria International Airport, with one or two stops on the way.

He wouldn't have minded paying for the private jet, but Mendenhall Security had insisted on paying for it because they considered Marie of high value, and therefore, her family was too.

High value? How?

Logan did not consider himself an inquisitive man, but this was his wife—uh, ex-wife—whose real job seemed to be a black hole to him. Why?

Before they reached their own ride, Logan turned to look at the royal family one last time, to the two bodyguards now walking toward their respective vehicles.

Zaid opened the front passenger side door—

Jerked back.

And collapsed to the ground.

People started screaming around Logan as the SUV carrying Aliyah and Abdul sped off.

"Take Jonas back to the ship!" Marie started running. "Now!"

Logan glanced back at the parking lot, just as Aliyah's second SUV swerved around them and screeched across the parking lot after the first SUV.

Marie was running toward Zaid on the ground.

For a second, bile formed in Logan's throat, and he felt a pang of...

Jealousy?

Nearby, the driver's side door of the Mendenhall Security SUV opened, and someone stepped out. A woman taller than Marie, dressed all in black. She knelt down and started to remove Zaid's vest.

Someone jostled against Logan. He stepped to the side as several of Zaid's men rushed down the gangplank toward their downed team member.

"Ladies and gentlemen, please return to the ship for your safety and security." The public announcement was so loud that it startled Logan.

Shipboard security came down the gangplank, ushering everyone to get back into the ship. Logan held Jonas's hand tightly.

"What's going on, Daddy?" Jonas walked as

fast as he could to keep up with Logan. "Where's Mommy?"

Logan didn't answer him. If his left arm weren't in a cast, he could have swept up Jonas and carried him in his arms.

"Walk faster, Jonas." Logan almost dragged him.

"I want Mommy!"

"Not now, Son. Let's go. Mommy is coming."

Is she? Logan wasn't sure. He could pray she would.

And he did.

CHAPTER THIRTY-EIGHT

*V*ehicles from the Victoria Police Department surrounded Marie and Esperanza in the parking lot, their flashing lights indicating to the arriving ambulance where to pick up a barely alive Zaid, whose life the duo had saved.

God saved his life.

Marie and Esperanza had stepped aside as the emergency medical responders took over.

A couple of officers approached Zaid's men, and one more came to talk to Esperanza. She was quite a sight, with blood all over her hands and jacket.

Marie looked at her own hands, smeared with Zaid's blood.

Why can't this vacation be uneventful?

Marie prayed to God for the safe return of Aliyah and Abdul as the ambulance sped away with Zaid and one other bodyguard.

When the police officer had finished recording Esperanza's statement, he turned to Marie. "You're with Mendenhall Security too?"

"No, sir. INTERPOL. I'm on vacation."

"Some vacation, eh?" The officer remained stoic. "Tell me what happened."

As much as she could recollect, eyewitness Marie did. As to who might have done it, Marie had no idea, though that would not be part of her statement. Observations were best reserved for the investigators, whoever they might be.

There was nothing more to say.

Clearly, the royal family had enemies. How they found out where Aliyah and Abdul were today was another matter altogether. Marie didn't get any sense that the royal family was trying to keep their cruise a secret. Abdul had been everywhere in public—on the cruise ship, in Juneau, Skagway, Ketchikan, and Victoria.

Granted, Aliyah and her assistant wore their hijab every day, but Abdul and the male security guards did not.

Whatever it was, Marie was sure that Zaid's team had taken the utmost precaution.

Yeah, before Wednesday happened.

What if Marie's presence onboard had triggered something?

"One inch to the right, and his neck would've been severed." Esperanza opened the back door of her SUV.

Four or five years ago, that statement would have made Marie flinch.

"They missed because the vehicle was moving and Zaid ducked." Esperanza pulled off her blood-soaked jacket and tossed it into a rectangular plastic bin. She pulled a couple of sheets of hand wipes from a container and handed them to Marie.

"Faster than a speeding bullet." Marie wiped Zaid's blood from her palms and then spot-cleaned her blouse and pants.

"God wants him to live." Esperanza put on a clean jacket that looked exactly like the stained jacket she had discarded. "Go get your family. We have a plane to catch."

Marie didn't move. "I can't help thinking..."

Around them, police vehicles started to leave. A few officers went up to the ship. Marie thought they were probably getting statements from eyewitnesses.

She figured Logan and Jonas were safe onboard. If Mrs. Ping was with them, she would keep them both safe. That was the main reason Marie had hired the seemingly unassuming fifty-something.

"It's not your fault," Esperanza kept her voice low. Police cars were still in the parking lot. "I looked them up. The boy's father has many enemies—including relatives. Did you know that the boy is eighth in line to the sultanate?"

"Whoa. No wonder security was tight." Marie's heart sank. "And then I showed up."

"Don't give yourself too much credit." Esperanza closed the vehicle door. "Stop looking so worried. We have bigger problems than this."

"What if my own son had been abducted?"

"Well, he wasn't. We don't deal with hypothesis right now, okay? Let the police do their job. You and I, we need to talk about Mr. B."

Marie had to switch gears for a quick minute.

"On the drive here from the airport, I found out that we know where he is." Esperanza's voice was low.

The parking lot was empty save for two police cars and a row of empty tour buses parked away from Esperanza's SUV. All the passengers were still onboard the ship until the police cleared them to go on land.

Buchanan. "I want in on it. I want this over and done with."

Catching Buchanan was the only way her family could be safe.

However, Marie had given her word to Logan and Jonas that she would be with them until Sunday before going back to work. The only way she could go with Esperanza once they dropped off the two of them was to get Mrs. Ping to fly home today as well.

I hate to spoil her garden walk with her new boyfriend.

"I thought you wanted to spend the weekend with your family," Esperanza added.

"I'll talk to Logan."

Esperanza took a deep breath. "Let me handle Mr. B. If you get involved, your boss is going to ask questions."

"Then I'll quit and go with you."

"You won't have a job when you come back though."

"I'll find work. I'll get a teaching certificate and teach foreign language at a school somewhere. Maybe even Jonas's school."

"You've thought about that, haven't you?"

"I've thought about many things."

Esperanza smiled. "Go get your family. I'll wait in the vehicle."

"Is it safe for you to sit out here?"

"Bulletproof."

"Seriously? How did you get this SUV on the island?"

"Borrowed it from a friend in Vancouver. He ferried it over this morning. I need to return it by noon. He wants it bleached-cleaned. Can you believe it? Where does he think I'm going to find the time?"

It was ironic to Marie that Esperanza could say that even as her cargo pants still had streaks of blood on them.

Esperanza must have seen what she was staring at.

"It's Zaid's blood," Esperanza assured her. "He's healthy and has no diseases."

"How did you—never mind. I don't need to know."

"You do know. All the photos and videos you sent from the cruise ship helped us to identify who they are, but not until last night."

"That explained why you came to get us in person."

"Well, I wanted to be sure your family is safe. If

they're safe, it will make it easier for me to offer you a job."

"The same one you tried to offer me three years ago?" Marie asked.

"I've fired too many people since then," Esperanza said. "That position now belongs to you, should you decide to take it."

"Can I take a raincheck? I need more time to think about it. This has been an interesting week."

"Sure thing. Fortunately, nothing happened to your family today. I pray that the outcome will be good for the royal family too."

Marie nodded. "Let me run back to the ship to shower and change?"

"Meanwhile I'll check how the car chase is going." Esperanza was already on her phone. "Don't take too long."

"I won't." Marie walked back to the ship while texting Logan.

CHAPTER THIRTY-NINE

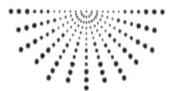

*M*rs. Ping had taken Jonas to the playroom, which was opened up for the kids after security ushered everyone back to the ship following the incident in the parking lot.

Incident?

Jonas's friend and his mother had been abducted. It could have been Jonas or anyone—

Well, maybe not.

Those thoughts percolated through Logan's head as he locked his stateroom door after the steward had dropped off their luggage. There were three pieces, plus Jonas's backpack.

Logan lay down on the sofa, shoes still on, and rested his free arm over his forehead. His other arm, still in a cast, stuck to his side uncomfortably.

I didn't ask for this, Lord.

There was nothing for him to do now but wait until the captain informed everyone that they could leave the ship.

The PA system came alive, startling him.

"Ladies and gentlemen, this is your captain speaking. If you saw what happened in the parking lot this morning, would you please make your way to the lounge?"

Logan suspected that the local police would like to speak with eyewitnesses. He had seen something, but it was from a distance. If he talked to the police, he would have to say that Marie ran to offer assistance. Then they would ask him who Marie was, and he'd have to say, "I don't know."

And that's the truth.

I have no idea what she really does to make a living.

All sorts of suspicions peppered Logan's mind, ranging from Good Samaritan to Really Bad Person and everything in between.

If Marie did not tell him about her other job, they could never reconcile as a couple because they would not be on the same page.

It had gone back three, five, six years now, and she hadn't come clean about her past or her present.

Therefore, there would be no future for them together.

"I'm a simple businessman—well, a fortuitous one—but she knows who I am, what I do, everything," Logan said aloud to no one. "I'm an open book, but she is a Pandora's box."

Somewhere in between disappointment and sadness, Logan feared knowing what was in her Pandora's box.

Slowly, Logan sat up.

I better go to the lounge.

Before he reached the door, a text message arrived from Marie. She wanted to know where Jonas was and where they had put her suitcase.

Logan decided to wait for Marie to show up because she did not have the key to his stateroom.

The knock on his door made Logan recall the night they had been attacked in Marie's stateroom. It had been an intense time for him, until the shipboard security personnel knocked, pretending to deliver their sandwich and snacks, which they hadn't ordered.

Logan's hands trembled. They had never trembled before, not even in billion-dollar merger meetings. Why were they trembling now?

One word: Marie.

Logan breathed in and out, praying for God to

calm his nerves. He made his way across the carpeted floor, looked through the peephole, and opened the door for Marie.

She had streaks of blood on her olive-green blouse—

Olive green.

He hadn't noticed it all morning. Why hadn't he noticed the color of her blouse? Shouldn't details matter when a man loved his woman...

Yes. That's right. I do love her in spite of everything.

"I need to shower and change my clothes," Marie said.

Logan invited her in. "I'm glad you're okay."

"No questions for me?" Marie stepped into the stateroom.

"Later." Logan pointed to her suitcase on the floor near the door.

"Thanks. Will you go get Jonas? Our flight is waiting."

"That might have to wait a bit. The captain just announced that eyewitnesses need to go to the lounge. I'm assuming police officers are waiting for us there."

Marie nodded. "I've already given my statement in the parking lot."

"Your friend too?"

"Yes. She saved Zaid's life before the paramedics arrived."

"Good." And he meant it.

"I'm sorry to run to the scene, leaving you and Jonas—but I know you'll take care of our son, as you always have."

Is that a compliment? "God protected us. I hope they find Abdul and his mother."

"The Victoria Police are on it."

"Do we know what's going on?" Logan asked.

"Not entirely. I doubt if they'll tell us, you know?" Marie rummaged through her suitcase, looking for clothes.

"Some secrets are meant to be kept."

"What?" Marie walked toward the bathroom.

Logan wondered if she heard him or was just playing ignorant.

"You better run to the lounge," Marie said. "You saw what happened. You saw Zaid go down. Anything you can tell the police will be helpful."

"If they ask me about you?"

"No worries. They already know who I am."

"But I don't," Logan said, but Marie had already shut the bathroom door.

CHAPTER FORTY

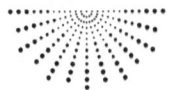

*W*hen they reached the Victoria International Airport, Marie received a message from the INTERPOL National Central Bureau in Ottawa that the car chase was over, and the two bodyguards who had abducted Aliyah and Abdul were dead from suicide by police.

Poor Hamza. Why did he do it?

Esperanza then told Marie that Zaid was in surgery for the gunshot wounds in his neck and shoulders, just where his Kevlar vest didn't cover.

"I'm glad you know CPR," Logan said upon hearing it.

Marie didn't reply. She knew that Logan was trying to adjust to all these things that a normal businessman would never have to deal with. She kept watching him, but not once since they had gotten into the SUV at the Victoria Cruise Ship Terminal and drove thirty minutes to the airport had he looked at her.

He seemed upset about something, and his demeanor worsened after he had given his eyewitness statement to the Victoria Police.

As for Marie, she had yet to get to her debriefing with INTERPOL Canada.

"I've seen worse," Esperanza said as they climbed up the stairs into the Gulfstream G280, one of Mendenhall Security's several jets.

This one would take them to Atlanta and, after that, Marie might have to leave right away with Esperanza to parts unknown. It could cost her job at INTERPOL, but at this point, she knew they had to take down Buchanan if her family were to live in peace henceforth.

Logan didn't need to know all that.

As soon as they boarded, Logan was looking for a place for Jonas to sit. Marie watched him busy himself checking out the two living areas. She assumed he hoped that Jonas could take a nap or play quietly without adults talking around him.

He's a good dad.

Mrs. Ping had tried to change her plans after

the events of this morning, but neither Marie nor Logan allowed her to do so. Marie still hadn't told Logan that she might not be able to stay in Atlanta the entire weekend. Marie would make her final decision at Logan's house.

The situation was fluid anyway. Esperanza had assured her that Mendenhall Security was on it. They might have news today, or they might not have any news until next week.

Marie waited for Logan and Jonas to return before she buckled in because she wanted to sit across from Logan, to look him in the eye, and maybe to assure him that all was well.

Who am I to give anyone assurance?

Only God can assure us of anything.

However, when Logan returned, he sat across from Jonas. The jet only had one seat on each side of the aisle, leaving no room for Marie to sit beside or across her ex-husband.

Marie didn't want to read too much into it, but was it possible for two people who loved each other to never be together again? She felt like he had died and left her—or rather, that she had died and left him.

Is this how grief really feels?

Marie checked Jonas's seat belt.

"I fastened it," Logan said to her.

"I know. I'm finding an excuse to give my son a hug." Marie kissed Jonas on his forehead. "Mommy loves you very much and will always love you. Do you know that?"

Jonas nodded. "I'm glad you're coming home with us, Mommy."

"Me too." But for how long?

"Do you have go back to work?" Jonas asked.

Did he mean at all? "Yes."

"When?"

"I don't know. But now I'm here."

Without warning, Jonas pinched Marie's arm nearest him.

"Oww!" Marie pulled her arm away. "What did you do that for?"

"Now you know you're here." Jonas nodded, eyes big and innocent.

Marie could hear Logan chuckle.

"Is that how you raised our son?" Marie joked.

Logan shrugged. "He never pinched me."

Marie had no comeback for that. Her arm was still stinging from that little pinch. Jonas had strong fingers. Maybe it was time for him to take piano lessons.

She had no idea how that popped into her head, but she could see him playing the old piano in her parents' house in Marseilles—like she used to do when she was about his age. She had taken piano lessons since the age of four, though she stopped playing any musical instruments after college.

Marie wished for her son more innocent days and comfort in life. That was all she wanted for her family. When she married Logan, she thought they'd have happily-ever-after seasons in the sun. But the rain fell, the storms came, and...

And here we are.

Marie sat down in her seat across the aisle from Jonas. She wondered if she should move elsewhere so she wouldn't be facing Logan, but he had his eye mask on, as if shutting her out.

Maybe I shouldn't read too much into that.

Marie looked out the window until Esperanza walked past her. She didn't say a word, but by the duffel bag she was carrying, Marie guessed that she was heading toward the shower at the back of the jet to change out of her clothes.

Marie didn't like to see Esperanza walking about in front of Jonas, still wearing her outfit that had blood stains on it. However, it was black material, and Jonas probably didn't notice. Besides, Esperanza said that Zaid was healthy.

So what if it's healthy blood? Blood is blood.

CHAPTER FORTY-ONE

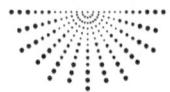

By the time they landed at Briscoe Field in Gwinnett County, Georgia, it was nearly midnight. Logan's chauffeur had been waiting for over an hour to pick them up.

Jonas was asleep on Logan's shoulder as they climbed down the steps. Logan let his chauffeur handle their suitcases, including Marie's.

It had been the quietest five-hour flight from Victoria to Atlanta. Logan had tried to nap under his eye mask, but he ended up praying the entire time. For some reason, all the work he had brought with him on the cruise didn't matter anymore. All that mattered to him on the flight was that his broken family had remained broken.

Had it been too much to ask of Marie to tell

him the truth about everything? Were there couples who kept secrets from each other for years—or the rest of their lives? How did that work out?

Logan decided he had to let Marie go.

In fact, he didn't want her staying with them this weekend. He wanted her to get a hotel room nearby. He'd even pay for it. She could come over to visit with Jonas on Saturday and Sunday before she went back to France on Sunday night. She had visitation rights, but Logan decided it was best not to welcome her back to his house.

His house.

That used to be their home.

Jonas stirred as Logan buckled him into the booster seat.

"Mommy?" Jonas rubbed his eyes. "Mommy?"

"I'm here." Marie stood outside the SUV door, smiling.

Funny how we want to put on our best faces for our children. Logan stepped aside to let Marie get to Jonas.

"Sit with me, Mommy." Jonas pointed to the empty seat next to him. "Daddy can sit in front with Mr. Wall Russ."

"Walrus?" Marie asked.

"It's Wallace, ma'am," the chauffeur said from the driver's seat.

"What I said, Wall Russ!"Jonas frowned. "He has tusks!"

"No, he doesn't," Logan said. "Please be polite to Mr. Wallace. He's going to take you to kindergarten in a couple of months."

"Why can't Mommy take me?" Jonas reached for Marie's arm.

"Because she has to go back to work," Logan said. He chided himself for speaking for Marie, but wasn't it the truth? She wouldn't be around after Sunday.

"Someday, Jonas," Marie said. "For now, we're going to get you home and get you to bed. Tomorrow you can show me your new toys in your playroom."

"Okay." Jonas smiled. "I love you, Mommy."

"I love you too, sweetheart." Marie's voice cracked.

Logan's heart broke.

~

*L*ogan's plan for Marie to stay in a nearby hotel didn't work out when his genetically stubborn five-year-old called the shots even before they reached home. Jonas had pitched a hissy fit in the car when he heard that his mother wasn't going to stay with them that night.

"But we're a family!" Jonas cried.

"I'll come to see you in the morning," Marie said.

"Noooooo."

Marie glanced at Logan.

Logan felt so ashamed that he had failed as a father to discipline this brat. At the back of his mind, he wondered if part of it had been Marie's fault. Wouldn't an absentee mother be damaging to a child's life?

"We have so many empty rooms, Daddy," Jonas tried again. "Why can't Mommy sleep in one of those rooms?"

That made Logan feel even worse.

"You don't have to see her, Daddy. We'll stay out of your way."

And there it was.

"You're not in my way, Jonas," Logan said.

"But Mommy is?"

Logan glanced back from his front passenger seat. Marie tried not to look at him.

Behind Logan's seat, he felt a kick.

"Stop that," Logan said.

"If I stop, will you let Mommy stay with us?" Jonas asked sweetly.

"Held hostage by a kid," Marie finally said.

"A hos—horse?" Jonas asked. "I want a horse too. And Mommy!"

"Your kingdom for a horse?" Marie laughed.

Logan said nothing. His parenting was a disaster, but his husbandhood was worse. In the middle of it all, he wondered if Jonas needed some help with his hearing. How could anyone morph the word *hostage* into *horse*?

Marie patted her son's knee. "Why don't we discuss this when we get home, okay? We don't want to distract Mr. Walrus—I mean Wallace—when he is driving at night."

Jonas nodded. "Are you wearing your seatbelt, Mr. Wall Russ?"

"Yes, sir." The chauffeur sounded serious. "We will be home soon, Mr. Horse."

"I'm not a horse!" And with that, Jonas moved on from his parents' problems.

CHAPTER FORTY-TWO

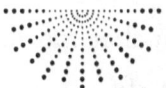

*B*y the time Esperanza sent Marie a message about Buchanan, it was shortly after her early dinner with Jonas on Saturday. Marie had spent the entire day being a stay-at-home mom for her son, and she cherished every minute of it.

"Best birthday present ever, Mommy!" Hyper Jonas cheered as he pushed another toy car down the track that he and Marie had constructed all around the basement playroom.

"You mean this race track?" Marie asked, as she eyed the wall of windows leading to the terrace and the backyard.

Jonas nodded. "You and me. We put it together."

"Yes, we did." Marie closed the blinds. It was dark outside, and someone could be in the yard—

No.

Nobody's in the yard except Espy's people.

Esperanza had sent only four people to guard the twenty-acre estate. Logan had an argument with Marie about it that morning after breakfast—which Marie had made.

Marie had a feeling that Logan was trying to pry information out of her. His questions were invasive, pushing her to a corner.

"Did you get enough sleep?" Marie tried to deflect his interrogation.

"Don't change the subject." Logan threw down his napkin on the table.

By then, Jonas had gone downstairs to play by himself, something he was used to.

It was only eight in the morning, and already the divorced couple had argued—but at least it was away from their son.

"Many things aren't adding up," Logan said. "If you don't tell me what's going on, you can tell Esperanza I don't want her people all over my property."

"It's for Jonas's protection."

"What about me?"

"You too."

"You don't trust me." Logan threw down his napkin and walked out of the beautiful French kitchen that he had renovated six years before for Marie.

Minutes later, Marie heard the garage door open.

It had been twelve hours, and Logan hadn't returned.

He had left her with Jonas.

"Mommy?" Jonas handed her a toy car. "A gift for you."

It was a red sports car.

"For me?" Marie smiled as best she could.

"Uh-huh. When you go to work, you can think of me." Jonas patted Marie on her shoulder.

Marie's eyes watered. "I'll carry it with me everywhere I go."

"Good idea! You want another car? How big is your backpack?" Jonas looked around.

"This is enough. More than enough." Marie put the car into the pocket of her shorts.

She didn't hear anyone come into the play-room, but when she looked up, there he was, standing at the door and watching mother and son.

"You got a car too?" Logan asked. He was sipping a bottle of mineral water.

"Daddy, you're home!" Jonas jumped up and tripped on the race track.

As if by instinct, Marie leapt into action and grabbed Jonas before he fell face first on the carpet.

"That was fast," Logan remarked.

Marie didn't say anything. She watched Jonas hug Logan. She had no doubt in her mind that Logan loved his son.

But does he love me still?

"What else can you do that we don't know about?" Logan's voice was icy cold.

"Are you picking a fight with the mother of your child in front of him?" Marie asked.

"I don't know. Is this a fight?" Logan threw the empty bottle into a trashcan.

"I want to fight too!" Jonas tugged at Logan's shirt. "I have boxing gloves."

"It's going to require more than boxing gloves." Logan laughed. "Well, young man, it's past eight o'clock at night. I assume you already had your dinner. It's time for you to go to bed. We have church in the morning."

"I want Mommy to tuck me in and pray with me," Jonas said.

"Okay. After you brush your teeth and change into your pajamas."

"I want Mommy to help me."

Logan glanced at Marie. "If she knows what to do."

Marie tried not to react.

"Of course Mommy knows what to do. We built this entire track all by ourselves." Jonas waved his arms around to show Logan the extensive race track that spread from one side of the room to the other.

"You two got carried away, didn't you?"

"Carried away?" Jonas looked puzzled. "We stayed right here in this room all day, Daddy. Nobody carried us away."

Marie wondered how often Logan left Jonas with Mrs. Ping. Logan worked a lot, even when they had been married. Now, even more so with the new business transactions that Logan's cousin Jared kept putting on his table.

Marie didn't ask him about his work. She hoped Logan wouldn't ask about hers.

But he had.

And he wasn't satisfied with any answer she had given him.

CHAPTER FORTY-THREE

"Jonas, you be a good boy and take care of Daddy, okay?" Marie was sitting at the edge of Jonas's full-size bed.

Her back faced Logan, so he could not see her face. He could clearly see Jonas. His head rested on the pillow, and he was wearing his favorite pajamas.

Logan kept his distance at the bedroom door, listening to every word.

"Mommy?" Jonas's lips quivered. "Don't go."

"I'm still here tomorrow."

"No, Mommy. Forever." Jonas sniffled.

"I'll be back soon." Marie held her son's hand. "Will you wait for me?"

Jonas nodded. "When will you come back?"

"Soon."

"Christmas?" Jonas's eyes brightened.

"I'll try."

"Try your best? Daddy said if you don't try your best, you're not trying enough."

Marie nodded. "I always try my best. It's very hard sometimes. I keep pushing on when I think of you."

"What are you pushing on, Mommy?"

"I don't know."

"How do you not know what you're pushing? Did you close your eyes?"

Valid question. Logan smiled.

"My job, I guess," Marie said. "It's very hard."

"I have a job too," Jonas said.

"Yeah?"

Jonas nodded. "Yeah. I play all day."

"Is that a job?" Marie asked.

"Best job ever!"

Logan chuckled, giving away his presence.

Marie turned around. "Didn't know you were there."

"I was going to my room." But he didn't move.

"Daddy, will you pray with us?" Jonas pointed to the other side of his bed. "You sit there."

And of course, Jonas insisted that they hold hands.

Marie's hand was smooth and warm in his. Logan remembered all the good times they had.

And then the bad times.

He stiffened.

"Daddy, pray." Jonas made a face at him.

Logan didn't feel like praying, but if he let Marie do it, she might go for a short prayer, and then he would have to let go of her hand. He'd rather liked holding her hand right now.

He'd had a hard day. Sure, it was Saturday, but his cousin with the majority share of their company had gone and done the unthinkable: pour millions into a company whose CEO he had just met a month or two before.

There was nothing Logan could do to undo the process.

Except wait for a moment in the future to say, "I told you so."

"Daddy?" Jonas asked.

"What?"

"Pray?"

Logan had no words.

God, forgive me. I am so lost as to what to do with my company, my business relationship with Jared, and with my wife—ex-wife—here.

Marie cleared her throat. "Close your eyes, Jonas."

Jonas did, and so did Logan.

Marie squeezed his hand gently. Logan felt like she was saying, "It will all get better."

But only God can make all things better.

"Lord Jesus," Marie prayed. "Thank You for always being with us, no matter where we are in the world. You know all about us and yet You still love us. You care for us. You provide for us. You never let us down. You lead us to the green pasture beside still waters. You calm our nerves. You are our peace. We thank You for a wonderful week in Alaska. We thank You for family time. We ask that You give us all a good night's sleep tonight. Help us get up bright and early to read the Bible and get ready for church. Thank You, God, for everything. In Jesus' name, I pray. Amen."

Logan said *amen.*

Jonas didn't say a word.

Logan opened his eyes to find Jonas fast asleep. He gently let go of his hand, and so did Marie. However, Logan did not let go of Marie's hand, even though she tried pull it away.

"We need to talk," he mouthed.

She nodded.

Logan closed the door gently. Outside the

bedroom, Logan felt an urge to pull Marie toward him as he used to do when Jonas was a baby, but he didn't. Instead, he led Marie downstairs to his home office.

"Your office?" Marie stopped short of entering it.

"You've seen it before, but I figured that if we talk in my office, it will be more businesslike." Logan opened the door to let Marie in. "That way, you won't think I have ulterior motives. Let's clear the air once and for all, like two logical persons talking business."

"What business might you be referring to?" Marie sat down in one of the armchairs surrounding a coffee table.

"I don't know. CIA. State Department. INTERPOL. Take your pick." Logan sat down in the other armchair across from Marie. That way, they faced each other.

Marie looked stunned.

"You thought I don't remember that night in Alaska. I remember more than you think."

"All that is not your concern."

"And that's how it all began." Logan leaned back. His arm itched in the cast.

"If I tell you anything, you and Jonas will be in danger."

"Ah. A threat."

"Not mine, I can assure you that." Marie's voice remained calm, but Logan knew he would be pushing her buttons tonight.

"External pressure, you're saying."

"I can't say anything."

"Either way, we're already in danger. Remember Wednesday night at sea?" Logan reminded her. "They know us now."

Marie looked away. "I'm sorry about that."

"If your work is so dangerous, or puts our son in danger, then do you think we should make a new agreement for you never to see Jonas again?"

"What?"

"How else do we protect him?"

"Espy's team—"

"No. That won't last. How much do you think her team costs?"

"You're not paying for it."

"She is for now. But at some point in time, it will no longer be cost-effective. Then what?"

"If we find Buchanan, then it will be over," Marie said.

"What will be over?"

"This nightmare."

"What nightmare?"

Marie didn't reply.

"Tell me, Marie," Logan pleaded, but he couldn't give up now. "I deserve that much."

"We're no longer married to each other."

"This tore us apart."

"Did it?" Marie looked puzzled.

Logan stared.

"What?" Marie asked.

"Jonas makes that face too. Usually when he's halfway irritated or confused or both."

"Huh." Marie got up. "Well, I'm tired. It's been a long day. I'd like to go to bed. We have church tomorrow, as you said."

"It's only nine o'clock." Logan pointed to his watch.

"For you, maybe. But I need to reset my clock to Paris time."

"When can we talk about this?" Logan felt defeated.

"If we find Buchanan and I quit my job, maybe soon. Otherwise, never."

Logan was stunned. There was no way he was going to ever get through to Marie. He had lost her forever, hadn't he? He felt like something was stuck in his throat. He couldn't get another word out.

Helplessly, he watched her leave his office.

Sigh.

He turned off the lights, and dragged himself out into the hallway.

And there she was. Leaning against the wall, her face in her palms.

Hiding from the world?

Without calling her name, Logan went to her. She wasn't startled when he approached her. He held her in his arms, neither one saying a word.

Logan forgot all the things he was angry about. All the secrets she had been keeping from him. All the reasons she had to stay away from the son she clearly loved.

After a while, Marie looked up. "Logan?"

"Yes, my love?"

"Will you wait for me?" she asked. "When the time is right, I will tell you everything."

Logan closed his eyes and nodded. What other choice did he have? He was still in love with his ex-wife. Someday, they would be on the same page. Just not today.

When the time is right?

And when might that be? Logan didn't ask, lest he spoil their moment. Instead, he cupped Marie's face in his hands, his thumbs wiping away the tears streaking down her cheeks. "You're a tough cookie, and here you are, crying."

"Only for two people in the world."

"That so?"

Marie nodded.

"Am I one of them?"

Marie nodded again. She lifted up her lips, waiting.

And Logan gave her what she wanted.

CHAPTER FORTY-FOUR

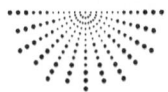

"*M*ommy, you must not lose the red car I gave you." Jonas's chubby finger pointed at Marie. "I want it back when you come home."

"Bossy, isn't he?" Marie turned to Logan.

Logan shrugged. He was standing in the foyer with them, waiting for Marie's ride. Any moment now, they all expected to hear the doorbell ring.

Esperanza had sent someone to pick up Marie and take her to Briscoe Field to fly out with Esperanza's team.

"Will you promise to wait for me?" Marie asked Jonas again, but it was perhaps also for Logan. They had halfway reconciled on Saturday night, but that was twenty-four hours ago.

After church and lunch, Marie had received a call from Esperanza. They had tracked Buchanan to Tunisia. If Marie wanted in on it, she could catch a ride out with the new members Esperanza had added to her team.

It came with a caveat.

There was no way Marie's supervisor in Lyon would agree to her involvement in any of this. For her own protection and that of her family, and the reputation of INTERPOL, Marie had to officially quit her job and go to work for Mendenhall Security.

That was her only guarantee she would have a job when the storm blew over.

Then again, while Mendenhall Security could guarantee that Marie would be compensated for her work as their newest polyglot translator, only God could guarantee her safety.

If He chose to.

If I die, I die. As long as my family is safe.

The bossy member of her family was still staring at her. Tears puddled in Jonas's blue eyes. He seemed angry and sad at the same time.

Marie had been there. Partings were such horrible times.

Marie sat down cross-legged on the marble

floor. Jonas sat on her lap. She held him there as he sobbed and sobbed.

"Jonas, you're now five years old and a big boy," Logan said. "You can handle this."

"I'm still Mommy's baby," Jonas replied.

Marie hugged him. "Yes, you are. And I'm going to give you another job."

"How much does it pay?" Jonas tried to deepen his voice.

Logan coughed.

Marie laughed. "What have you been teaching your son?"

"He's your son too."

The doorbell rang. Logan went to get it.

Jonas held Marie tighter. "Don't go! Don't go!"

"Jonas, your new job is to pray to God every day for Mommy until I come back to you," Marie said. "Can you do that?"

From the corner of her eye, Marie saw Mrs. Ping come down the hallway. She would be taking over as soon as Marie left.

"What should I pray for?" Jonas wiped his eyes.

"We can start with the fruit of the Spirit. That should take you nine days."

"I don't like all fruits. Only yellow kiwis."

"It's a metaphor—never mind. Daddy will tell

you what the fruit of the Spirit is. Won't you, Logan?" Marie looked up.

Logan had opened the door to a man in sunglasses.

"Hey Keenan," Marie said. "Meet Logan Urquhart, the father of my son."

Marie wasn't sure if it was a weird way to introduce her ex-husband, but the words went out of her mouth before she could edit them.

Logan tried to shake hands with Keenan O'Tierney, but the latter extended his left hand, making Logan do the same.

"So you work for Esperanza?" Logan asked.

"With her," Keenan replied. "We both own Mendenhall Security."

Marie let the men talk while she focused on Jonas. "Will you ask God to keep us safe?"

"And bring you back to me." Jonas hugged her. "You don't have to see Daddy if you don't want to. Come home to me, Jonas Ukulele."

"What?" Marie's eyes widened.

"You can live with me in the basement, Mommy. It's a big place, and we can play all day like yesterday."

Marie chuckled. "Jonas, remember that God cares for us and He loves us."

"Yes."

"God protects us no matter where we are. I will see you soon." Marie kissed her son on the top of his head.

"How soon?" Jonas Ukulele asked.

"Very soon."

"Very, very soon?" Jonas knotted his eyebrows together. Now he looked like Logan when the latter was concerned about something.

"Sooner than you think."

"I can think a lot, Mommy."

"I'll come back and we can see each other again. Wait for me, and pray that God will bring us back together again."

"God can do that?"

"Of course. God can do anything." Marie gave him another hug. "Mommy loves you very much."

"I love you first," Jonas said, his competitive streak showing.

"Technically, God loves us first."

"He did?"

"Yep."

"Do you love Daddy too?" Jonas asked.

That was an unexpected question.

The atmosphere in the foyer stilled. The two men at the door stopped talking.

Marie assumed that Logan was probably waiting to hear her answer too.

Maybe it was time to start telling the truth, and face the truth about their lives together and apart.

"Yes, Jonas," Marie confessed. "I've always loved your daddy."

Logan cleared his throat.

Marie ignored him. "Now, Jonas. I have one more job for you."

"Wow! Two jobs!" Jonas put up four fingers. "I'm going to be rich!"

"Rich in heavenly things," Marie corrected him.

"What's the other job?"

"Will you keep an eye on your daddy? He needs you." Marie got to her feet and patted Jonas's head.

"One eye?" Jonas asked. "What about the other eye?"

"What?"

"You said to keep one eye on Daddy. What do I do with the other eye?"

Marie glanced at Logan, who didn't say a word. Keenan was also watching her trying to respond to this child. "Let me rephrase that. Will you take care of Daddy while I'm at work?"

"Sure!" Jonas spread out his hands. "He doesn't have a job. Mostly he sits and stares out the window."

Logan coughed.

"I'll wait in the car," Keenan said and exited the door.

"Does he?" Marie held Jonas's hand and walked him to the front door.

"Yep! Maybe I can share my two jobs with him." Jonas looked at Logan. "Daddy, do you need a job?"

Logan kept a straight face. "You got one for me?"

"It pays a lot!"

"Does it?"

"Uh-huh. Mommy's going to come home to check on us, so we better behave."

Logan glanced at Mrs. Ping.

The nanny took Jonas's hand from Marie. "I bought five flavors of ice cream, but they don't have vanilla. Can you believe it?"

"Wow!" Jonas jumped up and down. "Five *favors*! Five *favors*! Can I have all five?"

"If Mommy and Daddy say you can," Mrs. Ping replied.

Marie looked at Logan. "Oh, I don't know. Five in one sitting? I mean, cavities and all."

Logan pretended to think deeply.

"Daddy, please? I have to eat them now before they melt!"

"What do you think, Mommy?" Logan asked Marie.

"Maybe only today. Then he can spread out each flavor for the rest of the week."

"That makes sense." Logan nodded. "All right, go with Mrs. Ping. Let her scoop them out for you, okay?"

"Thank you! Bye!" Jonas was skipping away in the direction of the kitchen, as Mrs. Ping tried to keep up with him.

"So easily distracted," Marie said.

"Who would think we'd lost to ice cream." Logan shook his head.

"Don't use it as a treatment," Marie warned. "I don't want him to become overweight."

"He wears it off playing with his friends. I'm thinking he should play soccer or something soon. Get all that energy out of his system."

"Soccer?" Marie was alarmed. "Haven't you heard of brain injuries?"

"You mean football?"

"Both. Let him play something more benign."

"Like what?"

"Piano or something."

"Piano? No one has played our Steinway grand since you left." Logan reached for Marie's hand.

"You'll have to come home so that we can discuss it."

"About sports?" Marie let Logan pull her gently toward him.

"And other things..." Logan nuzzled her hair.

"What other things?"

"I don't know. We'll think of something." Logan held her. "I miss you already."

I miss you too.

Marie couldn't say it. She didn't want to get his hopes up. She could not assure him that she would return from the battlefield against Buchanan.

She made a note to herself to update her will, just in case.

CHAPTER FORTY-FIVE

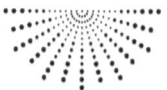

*M*arie fanned herself with a manila folder under the ceiling fan that had stopped working an hour ago. Someone was supposed to bring in box fans to help circulate the air in the stuffy operational center, but until then, they had turned down the partially working air conditioner.

The crowd of Mendenhall Security support personnel all around Marie in the giant room made it worse, as their collective body heat rose and swirled and assaulted her sensitive nose every minute. If she hadn't left her face mask in her hotel room, she'd be wearing it.

Sweat beaded on Marie's forehead and neck. She could use a glass of ice-cold water, but nobody had the time to go get her something. The refrigerator in the break room was broken, and no one was allowed to come and go from this location until Operation Buchanan was over.

The city of Benghazi was just outside the building, and Marie was sure they sold ice-cold water somewhere out there in the market. That seemed to be all she dreamed of, even though it was supposed to be ninety-something degrees this afternoon.

Not hotter than in here.

She reached for her cotton shirt she had discarded. The soaked-through shirt was hanging over the empty seat back next to hers—a seat vacated by Esperanza Diaz-Mendenhall, who had inserted herself into the fray only moments before.

Marie wiped her face with the shirt. It smelled of her own sweat and perfume. A bad combination for such a hot July day. Her sleeveless blouse stuck to her bra and torso.

Her manila folder fanned only hot air on her face. She felt faint.

Maybe if I go to the hallway...

Slowly, Marie got up. She walked past a bank of windows that were shut and sealed like the seams of a casket. She felt no breeze at all. Somewhere north of this building, the Gulf of Sidra danced in the wind of the Mediterranean.

While we are dying in this tomb...

Her hand reached for the window latch, even as her mind knew it was forbidden. Cracking a window would let the entire region of Cyrenaica know that the Americans had arrived—albeit to excise their common enemy, that arms dealer extraordinaire, that had evaded authorities for five years and ran with global terrorists such as Molyneux, evil personified.

How could Buchanan have been so elusive?

His coat of many colors had given him nine lives. Originally from South Africa, his father was Scottish and his mother of unknown origins. How Buchanan ended up as a businessman in the Middle East, dining with sultans, princes, and heads of state, was anyone's guess.

The love of money, maybe?

Soon, he moved on from state dinners to backroom breakfasts with Yemeni terrorists, bartering oil and gold for bullets and missile launches.

Then he wandered into the lair of one Molyneux—and that was how he ended up on the radar of the FBI and INTERPOL, inside their operation to capture the elusive terrorist before she blew up yet another city.

Assigned to translate *in situ*, Marie was caught up in that web of intrigue involving FBI agents in deep undercover, although her involvement resulted in new friends, among whom was Esperanza.

Thank God for Esperanza!

The widowed security specialist had done so much for her family, to keep them safe in Atlanta while Marie was busy at work and could not protect them herself. When all this was over, Marie could go home to protect her family herself.

Home?

Family?

Did I just hear myself say that?

She shut the door behind her and leaned on the plaster wall. It was cool to the touch. When she felt warm, she moved a foot to the right and leaned against the wall again, to siphon heat off the wall. She knew she looked weird, but she was feeling very hot right now.

She stared down the hallway.

Half the lights were out.

Why?

She turned her face the other way. No one was there.

It was eerily quiet.

I'm overthinking again.

Marie closed her eyes.

When she opened them again, Esperanza was

standing in front of her, waving a bottle of cold water at her.

"Thank you! Thank you!" Marie grabbed the plastic bottle and drank it.

"You're aware that you're drinking micro-plastic," Esperanza said.

"Or die?"

"Good point."

"What's the situation?" Marie placed the bottle against her cheeks and neck, letting the cold condensation on the wall of the plastic cool her down.

"We're still waiting."

"Waiting. That's all we do, it seems."

Esperanza nodded. "This will be over soon, and you'll be with your family again in no time."

"I have to tell Logan." *I wish I could tell him everything.*

"Not what's in the past, but you can if you work for me." Esperanza tilted her head. "Made your decision yet?"

Marie sipped water slowly.

If it hadn't been for Esperanza, INTERPOL would not have known that the private investigator whom Logan sent to Europe to find Marie had entangled himself with Buchanan. The PI had seen an opportunity to make a quick buck, and nearly lost his life in the process. He could never tell anyone what really happened three years before in Europe. It explained the lack of forthrightness the PI had with the man who had hired him and paid for all his expenses.

Once again, Logan would be left in the dark.

Yet, he and Marie had Esperanza to thank for their safety. It had been Esperanza who had sent a decoy to throw off the real scent of Marie's whereabouts, leading the PI to dead ends.

Now Marie knew that Esperanza had done all that as a gesture of good faith.

And a carrot to get Marie to work for Mendenhall Security.

Two months after the PI went home to the United States, they lost Buchanan again. Marie filed for divorce to distance herself from Logan and her beloved son. Using the divorce settlement, she paid Esperanza's company to protect Jonas and Logan for a year—until word came to her that Buchanan was killed in Yemen.

Two years later, Marie found out on their family cruise in Alaska that the news of Buchanan's death had been false.

Esperanza's secure phone buzzed. "What? Who?"

Marie finished drinking her water. Maybe she

shouldn't have gulped it down, but whatever. She turned to return to the operational center as Esperanza was still on the phone, but the latter stopped her.

She hung up. "Your ex-husband relayed a message to my office in Misty Mountain."

"Logan?" Marie asked.

"Is there another ex I don't know about?" Esperanza asked.

"What does he want?" Marie didn't know why Logan would try to contact her, but she recalled the last day they had been together, when he told her he missed her already. They were standing on the foyer of his house on Paces Ferry in Atlanta.

"He wants to know how to send you a care package," Esperanza said.

"Seriously?"

"Yeah. The man's in love."

Marie didn't know how to respond to that. "You got that out of a phone message?"

"You must have had a good time on the cruise—aside from the incidents."

"Before Buchanan showed up and ruined our party." Marie breathed in deeply.

"We're going to take care of him. Don't you worry."

At the end of the hallway, a door opened and

about four or five people in combat gear marched in.

"Our reinforcements have arrived." Esperanza went to greet them.

MI5.

Marie knew that the United Kingdom Security Service was after Molyneux. Buchanan was secondary to them. Even the United States Central Intelligence Agency thought that Buchanan would eventually give up Molyneux.

I fear they will all make a deal with Buchanan and let him go.

Marie's family would never be safe until Buchanan was behind bars or dead.

Perhaps Zaid's people would not let Buchanan go.

Marie began to pray.

CHAPTER FORTY-SIX

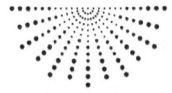

*C*rack!

"What's that?" Marie pressed her headset against her ears. The sound didn't repeat.

"Did you hear that?" she asked her colleagues in the operational center. This corner of the room was filled with translators and analysts with far more time in the battlefield than she had, but Esperanza had put Marie in charge because the head translator was out there with Esperanza.

The people nearest her shook their heads.

Crack-crack-crack!

"There!" Marie said.

"Got it."

Finally. Maybe we need better equipment.

Marie was already on to the next step, but she

could not get hold of the team across the street. "Eldorado? Come in, Eldorado?"

Team Eldorado did not respond.

Marie tried another channel. Still nothing.

Lord, please keep everybody safe.

She knew it was a blanket prayer, but that was all she could say right now. Even if she simply called to God, she knew that God would read her mind and hear her prayer. God was powerful like that. He knew all things, saw all things, heard all things.

Marie glanced at the next person over. Her screen was at least fifty-two inches, and she was tracking Team Eldorado through the live cam attached to the videographer embedded with Esperanza.

Marie's screen was filled with sound waves—

She heard a voice speaking Arabic.

She turned up the audio. Heard that voice again. More Arabic.

She hit the replay button and isolated the single sentence.

And she recognized him.

Zaid.

On the raid? No way.

"Someone get me Espy now!" Marie shouted.

In her headset, she heard more gunfire.

Distant explosions.

A crackle on Marie's headset startled her.

"Mikonos? Come in, Mikonos!" It was Esperanza.

Before Esperanza could say a word, Marie jumped in. "Espy, I heard Zaid's voice."

"What?"

"Where are you?"

"We retreated around the corner. Can't get in."

It wasn't Marie's place to respond, but she was thinking that the MI5 reinforcement didn't seem to help if Esperanza couldn't get into the building to extricate Buchanan himself—that was, if he was really in there.

They had been chasing Buchanan across the Middle East and North Africa since that day his voice appeared in Marie's stateroom on the cruise ship in Alaska. More than seven weeks later, intel led them to Libya. And here they were in Benghazi, a place of bad memories for the Americans.

The sounds of gunfire subsided.

"We're going back in," Esperanza said. "You sure about Zaid?"

"Tell him I say hello." Marie prayed again for the safety of the team.

She leaned to her right, and her colleague made

room at her workstation for Marie to watch the live camera.

Onscreen, Esperanza crossed the street in that dusty old town, straight toward Buchanan—if he was there at all.

The area had turned into a dystopian dust bowl few dared wander into in the last few years, more so than in decades past. The country was lost to anarchy, and the United States had pretty much abandoned it. In this nest of terrorists, Buchanan had found kindred spirits.

Buchanan had managed to bribe his way through the wasteland, dug into a safe hovel, and waited for a break in the dark clouds over him.

Radio silence.

All they had was video with no sound.

Marie's eyes were on the screen. It was hard to see much since the body cam was on the last person in the back. She tried to spot Zaid and his team.

Would Omar be there too or was he with Aliyah and Abdul back home? Since the Victoria Police had successfully rescued both of them from the abductors in June in the short car chase, Aliyah's husband had ordered the entire entourage to go home. Zaid had told Esperanza that much.

Marie couldn't imagine what the interaction

was like between Esperanza and Zaid, two competitive alpha leaders.

But why would Zaid be in Benghazi at all? Wasn't his role simply as a bodyguard to the young prince and his mother?

Shots rang out.

The screen went dark. It could mean many things—including perhaps that the translator had lost his body cam. Or that he was injured.

Marie prayed again. It was all she could do.

Praying was an automatic thing for her these days. She had prayed so much since she left Jonas, left Logan, left Atlanta. While they were in good hands with Mendenhall Security keeping them safe, Marie couldn't help but wish that she were there with them.

Praying was her only reprieve.

Well, truly, God was her only reprieve.

There was no communication from Team Eldorado for the next ten minutes until Marie heard Esperanza over her headset. She assumed everyone else heard her too.

"Looks like Buchanan." Esperanza's voice was calm. "A DNA test will confirm it."

The entire room cheered.

"Don't celebrate yet. He's still alive," Esperanza said. "Hey Marie?"

"Yes, ma'am?"

"Zaid says hello."

So he was there. Marie was quite confident they had really gotten Buchanan if Zaid was on it. That man seemed to be just as determined as Esperanza—if not more so—to get Buchanan.

Marie prayed that the worst was over. If they caught Buchanan, Esperanza would make sure he went to trial. If Zaid had anything to do with it, Buchanan was as good as dead.

All Marie could think of right now was Jonas. There was no doubt in her mind that if Buchanan escaped or was released, he would come after more than just Marie next time. He would come after her entire family.

If anything happened to Jonas, both she and Logan would be devastated.

If anything happened to Logan, Jonas would be fatherless. It would break Jonas's heart.

And mine too.

Yes, mine too.

CHAPTER FORTY-SEVEN

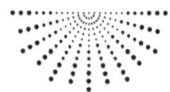

One month later, Logan found Jonas praying in his playroom. He was sitting among his toy cars and trucks, surrounded by tracks that meandered all over the floor.

"God, keep Mommy safe and Daddy sane." His voice was soft, almost in a whisper, but Logan heard him nonetheless.

Sane?

Where did Jonas learn that word?

Then again, Logan would be lying if he didn't admit that he was losing his sanity not being able to see Marie. She had been gone for two and a half months.

I miss her as though I would never see her again.

He wished he hadn't let Marie go three years

before. He regretted going through with the divorce.

What couldn't they resolve without separating from each other?

Couldn't they have met in the middle somewhere?

It stilled bothered him that Marie couldn't tell him what he wanted to know about her other job, the hush-hush one that she couldn't even talk about.

And her friend Esperanza—she didn't look like someone Marie had randomly met at the hair-dresser. She looked like she could kill.

The fact that Logan's house now had security guards twenty-four seven revealed a lot about where he and Marie were now: back to square one of unanswered questions.

Logan figured that all this could be over once they captured the Buchanan guy. That was one name he had caught during the Wednesday night attack outside the coast of Ketchikan. He must be some bad apple if so many international agencies were after him.

Logan waited for Jonas to finish his prayer.

The boy went on and on.

At some point, Logan closed his eyes and followed along.

"Help Mrs. Ping catch the captain. She said he's a whale." Jonas's eyes were shut tight. "She's going to need a big fishing rod."

A whale of a catch?

Logan wondered whether he should leave the child alone.

"All those people in our yard. They won't play with me." Jonas's voice broke.

Logan recalled what Marie said to him on the last day they were still onboard the cruise ship when it docked in Victoria.

He needs siblings to play with.

Poor Jonas. An only child who tried to befriend the Mendenhall Security guards stationed on Logan's property.

Mrs. Ping was more like a surrogate grandmother to him than a playmate.

What about the kids in kindergarten? They could come over and play with him? They had done so before—many times.

Still.

"Amen!" Jonas said the word so loudly that Logan's eyes snapped open.

"Daddy!" Jonas ran to him, tripping over his tracks.

He froze. Stared at the broken tracks, and began to cry.

"Shhhhh." Logan was on his knees. "Are you hurt?"

"No, but my tracks are." Jonas tried to fix the disjoined tracks.

"Let me help." It was easy.

"It's a boo-boo." Jonas inspected it.

"Does it need a Band-Aid?"

Jonas nodded.

Logan went to the small kitchenette to find the first aid kit.

"Two Band-Aids." Jonas held up five fingers.

"One big one is enough, don't you think?" Logan waved it in the air.

"I guess."

They taped the Band-Aid under the track where two parts met.

"Why not on top?" Jonas asked.

"Because we need a smooth surface for the car wheels to glide over."

Jonas shrugged. He yawned.

"Time for bed, Mr. Jonas." Logan crumpled up the Band-Aid cover and threw it in the trash can.

"I want Mommy to tuck me in."

Here we go. "Mommy is at work, but she'll be home soon. How about I tuck you in and we can pray for her?"

"Okay."

Logan made a quick work of their nightly process. Jonas brushed his teeth and climbed into bed. He read a passage from the children's Bible about Jesus feeding the five thousand.

Jonas was fast asleep before Logan finished praying.

After turning off the bedroom light, Logan went downstairs to do some work. He recalled trying to make Marie talk to him in a business setting in his office, as if that would work.

He heard music coming from the laundry room near the kitchen, and figured Mrs. Ping was still awake. Sure enough, Mrs. Ping was listening to music on her phone while folding Jonas's laundry. She looked pensive.

"You okay?" Logan asked.

She nodded.

"When are you going to see your grandkids?"

"In a week. I'll arrive one day before my youngest granddaughter celebrates his first birthday."

"If you need to take more time off..."

"No need." Mrs. Ping shook her head.

"You can leave a week sooner. Or later."

Mrs. Ping gave him a look.

Logan lifted up his left arm. "See a cast?"

"No." She looked puzzled.

"Neither do I." Logan dropped his arm. "It's been over two months. My arm has healed. It's not broken any more. I can handle my own son."

"Really?" Mrs. Ping kept picked another article of clothing from the dryer. "Can you survive Jonas without me for three weeks, Mr. Logan?"

"It's still Mr. Logan after all these years?" Logan asked.

"It's best if we keep a wall between us, even though I'm old enough to be your mother." Mrs. Ping placed the folded shorts neatly in the laundry basket at her feet.

"You've been a blessing to us," Logan said. "I need to give you a raise."

"You've given me a raise every year."

"Not enough, it seems."

"Now you're giving me three weeks off." Mrs. Ping knotted her eyebrows together. "You going to be okay that long without me?"

Logan nodded. "I'm on a staycation the entire time, remember? Plus, Polly does all the cooking, so we're not going to starve. I'm going to give Wallace some time off too, so I'll take Jonas to kindergarten."

"Okay." She still looked worried.

"You'll still have your job when you come back."

Mrs. Ping picked up the laundry basket. "I won't when Marie returns."

"If she does." Logan would love to see Marie in town, but not if it didn't make her happy.

"Won't she? She told Jonas she'll be back."

"To visit, yes. But I don't know if she will stay." Logan had spoken his mind, but he wasn't sure if that was too much to tell his son's nanny.

"Pardon my intrusion, Mr. Logan, but I thought you two got back together on the cruise."

What to say? "We had our moments, but they were mere moments, you know? It might be over for us."

"Maybe there's still something there."

"Marriage is hard." Their no-fault divorce was a case in point.

"Life is hard," Mrs. Ping said. "But all things are possible with God. Hope in Him for the best."

The best? Logan knew that the best partner for him was Marie. "She's all but disappeared. I sent a care package to Mendenhall Security, but I haven't heard back."

"If she's working, she's busy."

"Maybe she has moved on."

"Not Marie." Mrs. Ping sounded confident.

It made Logan curious. "Why do you say that?"

"She seems to be a one-man woman type."

"That so?" Curiouser and curiouser.

"I think she's still in love with you—care package or not."

Logan sighed. "We've hurt each other too much."

Mrs. Ping stopped at the door. "Sometimes we have to love unconditionally."

CHAPTER FORTY-EIGHT

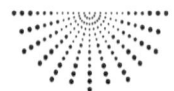

*A*fter two weeks, Logan's staycation routine became automatic for him. Wake Jonas up, read the Bible to him, get ready for school, feed him breakfast, drop him off at the kinder-garten, come home, putter around, pick up Jonas, take him to lunch, bring him home, play with him all afternoon or supervise playtime with his friends, feed him dinner, prepare him for bed, read the Bible to him, send him to bed, crash like an exhausted dad, and start all over again the next day.

Saturdays, they slept in all morning. Sundays, Logan set five alarms to get them both up and ready for church.

Midtown Chapel was about twenty minutes south in midtown Atlanta. The pastor had mentioned raising funds to plant a church in the North Georgia Mountains, but that would be even farther away from Paces Ferry Road.

Logan wished there was a church down the street from them that they both liked. Sure, there were many churches in the area, but he liked Midtown Chapel the best, in spite of the distance. Both the pastor and assistant pastors were thoughtful preachers.

Their children's program was top notch and biblically sound. Logan didn't want to pull Jonas from that environment.

This Sunday, the sermon was for Logan. Their senior pastor was out of town, so Assistant Pastor Byron Moss preached. The congregation laughed until they cried when Byron told the story of how he met his wife Tina for the first time when she was in Nassau to teach Vacation Bible School. They hated each other then. Two years later, they met afresh when Tina returned to the Bahamas.

Logan began to wonder if he could look at Marie "afresh." If they could start over, would they? Could they?

Byron went on to remind everyone to love one another with God's love, not human love. "You have all heard that God's love is sacrificial, but do you really know what that means for yourself, your own situation?"

Logan thought Byron was looking right at him. He turned his eyes toward the open Bible in his hand to avoid eye contact with the pastor, who also happened to be his friend. Logan made a note to himself to sit way in the back pews next Sunday.

"Ephesians 5:25 says, 'Husbands, love your wives, just as Christ also loved the church and gave Himself for her.' When Jesus Christ died on the cross for our sins, He gave himself for us. God sacrificed His only Son to save us."

Byron walked to the edge of the platform. "Jesus is my example of how I am to love Tina. That is, I am to love her more than I love myself. Am I doing that on a daily basis? Or is it just at my own convenience? It wasn't convenient for Jesus to sacrifice for us, was it? Yet, He did it out of love. Husbands, what does your love for your wife look like?"

Do I love Marie more than I love myself?

Logan wondered if he would be able to put up with Marie disappearing for months at a time, leaving their son with an absentee mother and a husband to sleep alone in their master bedroom? It would be almost like a long-distance relationship, and he wasn't sure he wanted one.

Byron went on to his next point. "God's love is unconditional."

Whoa. What Mrs. Ping said before she left for her vacation.

Logan looked to his left and right, and then back at his Bible. What was God trying to tell him?

"Let's read Colossians 3:19. 'Husbands, love your wives and do not be bitter toward them.' What does that mean to you?" Byron asked. "Are you angry with your wife? Bitter about something she's done to you? Unforgiving about the past?"

Again, Byron seemed to be staring right at Logan.

Am I bitter toward Marie?

Once upon a time, he had been. Now, not so much. After their Alaskan trip, Logan began to realize that he had to accept Marie for who she is. If she worked for INTERPOL—as that Buchanan guy said she did, which she hadn't denied—then Logan had to live with it.

Why couldn't he live with it? They'd have to adjust to their special relationship, like military spouses had to. It would mean many months of loneliness, but if Logan truly loved Marie, he would deal with it.

If he truly loved her...

After church, one of Jonas's friends wanted him

to go over to their house for a hamburger cookout. Logan went with him, accompanied by two men from Mendenhall Security.

By the time Logan reached home, Jonas was ready for his afternoon nap.

So was Logan, but he drank some coffee and padded to his office.

He knew it was still there in his safe, but he had to see it firsthand to make sure.

He punched in the combination to his safe, and reached in to get the box.

Yes, Marie's diamond ring and their wedding bands were still there. The rings they had bought together in Paris some six years before. The rings they had worn for three years into their marriage.

The rings he could not part with.

Logan closed the jewelry box and placed it on his oak desk. He leaned back against his office chair and closed his eyes.

Lord, please forgive me, and restore our marriage.

When he finished praying, he knew what to do.

Nervously, he texted Esperanza. He didn't want to send another care package. He wanted to talk to Marie, to hear her voice, and he wouldn't take *no* for an answer.

Of course, Marie wasn't available.

CHAPTER FORTY-NINE

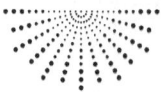

*B*efore Logan knew it, Monday and Tuesday came around again, and then Wednesday. He was back to his weekday routine. He would drop off Jonas at the kindergarten and then go to the grocery store. Except on Thursday.

On Thursday, he stayed in Jonas's class during the first period to talk about his job as a father. The teacher had asked if he was a stay-at-home dad. Finding out he wasn't, she asked him to speak to the kids anyway about what it took to raise a five-year-old. The entire time, Jonas was lying down on the rug, playing with his fingers and toes, not paying any attention to his dad's carefully prepared speech.

Then Logan went home only to realize that he

had worn mismatched socks to kindergarten, and that there was a dollop of organic mixed berry jam on his Balenciaga polo shirt.

He threw his clothes into the washing machine, and wished Mrs. Ping was back working in his house. She had started out as a nanny, but agreed to add on more work around the house for extra pay.

Thank God this was his last week of staycation.

Somehow he didn't miss Wallace as much. Without the chauffeur around, Logan could drive his other cars. Jonas was excited to be allowed in some of the sleek vehicles, which looked like his toy cars, except bigger and more expensive.

However, after being driven around in Logan's Bugatti La Voiture Noire, Jonas said he would rather be in his dad's Ford pickup truck than "all the sports cars in the world."

Good for you, son.

However, after grubby hands went all over the interior of the truck, Logan had to clean it up. That was Wallace's job, but he wasn't there.

This morning, Logan decided he would wash a few of his vehicles by himself. That was also Wallace's job, but he deserved the time off too.

As far as Logan knew, Wallace was probably at home, tending his vegetable garden. His lovely wife would never be short of squash and tomatoes and whatever else the couple loved to plant in their backyard.

As Logan gathered up things to wash and polish his truck, he wondered what Mrs. Ping was doing. She was supposed to fly from Florida, where her youngest granddaughter lived, to Victoria, British Columbia, where her latest boyfriend would meet her.

Somehow Mrs. Ping had kept up with the captain of the *Alaskan Queen of the Arctic Seas*, although this would be the first time those two would see each other since June.

More than Marie and me, I suppose.

Logan walked down the gentle slope next to his driveway to find the faucet and the garden hose. When he came up, there she was—wearing a light pink tee shirt, a pair of stonewashed jeans, and what looked like black combat boots—like she had just finished work, and changed only her blouse.

Or maybe, like she could run away in those boots if she had to.

Caught off-guard, Logan nearly slipped down the grassy slop, hose in hand.

"Logan." It was all she said.

"Marie." Logan couldn't speak beyond that.

I love you.

I miss you.

I hate being without you.

None of those words came out of his mouth.

"Marie," he said again, dropping his hose, and making his way toward her. He straightened up. "Are you here to help me wash my pickup truck?"

"What? You're putting me to work right away?" Marie smiled.

"Speaking of work, I thought you were in the middle of a project."

"I was. We finished early."

"Does that mean all is well?"

"For now."

"Are we safer?"

"You mean like you and me, or the world in general?" Marie asked.

"The world?" Logan didn't want to pry for details. He remembered Mrs. Ping's advice.

Sometimes we have to love unconditionally.

Perhaps Marie was the CIA-type. She couldn't tell anyone what her job was. At the very least, she worked for INTERPOL, and that was like the FBI. Agents had to be people of integrity, right?

Logan was confident that Marie wasn't a villain.

A villain?

Logan rolled his eyes. He had watched too

many cartoons with Jonas these past two weeks, for sure.

"Why?" Marie asked. "What's the matter? Why did you roll your eyes?"

"I was just thinking about the cartoons that Jonas and I have been watching."

"Distracted, aren't you?"

Logan cleared his throat. "You were saying?"

Marie didn't reply. She was looking at him. The brown specks in her eyes sparkled. Or maybe her eyes were moist. Logan couldn't tell. Dared not tell.

The way she looked at him reminded him of their wedding day on Cumberland Island, how the morning sun also shone in her eyes when they pledged their love for each other before God and family.

It reminded Logan of the love they had for each other.

"I'm happy to see you," he said. "I'm happy you're safe."

"Thank God for that. He was with us every step of the way, everywhere we go." Marie waited, as though to see how Logan would respond.

Logan would have in times past, but not today. Right now, all he felt was love for Marie.

He should not have let her go.

They stood in silence for too long, perhaps,

because Marie stepped back. "I have to talk to you about something."

"Let's go inside." He had to go inside. He wanted to open his office safe to take out the most precious thing inside. Oh, wait—the box was still on his office desk. He hadn't returned it to the safe since Sunday. He had stared at its content every day at least once since then.

Marie pointed to the garden hose on the ground. "I thought you were going to wash your truck."

"It can wait. I'll wash it later, maybe after I pick up Jonas from school. He's going to rub his sticky hands all over it anyway." Logan paused. "Right now, I have something to show you."

"What is it?"

"It's in my office." Logan held Marie's hand.

"You didn't know I was coming."

"No, but I knew I was going to show it to you whenever I see you. And here you are."

"And here I am." She let him lead her. "I was going to suggest we talk in your office also, but after we wash your truck—although it's a better idea to wait until after school."

"Maybe Jonas can help," Logan said.

"Right."

And they laughed.

CHAPTER FIFTY

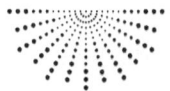

"*W*ant something to drink?" Logan asked as he ushered Marie into his office.

"No, thanks. I just had a late breakfast flying in, and too much coffee." Marie made her way to the plush sofa across the coffee table from the two armchairs that they had sat in three months before.

She watched Logan walk around his big desk. He didn't say a word.

Her watch chimed. She turned it off.

When she looked up, Logan was walking toward her. He knelt down in front of Marie.

"What are you doing?" Marie could barely speak.

Between Logan's fingers was a familiar-looking diamond ring.

Marie held her breath.

"You know that I love you. I should never have let you go. I should have fought for you, for our marriage."

Marie didn't know what to say. He looked like he meant every word.

"Do you still love me?" Logan asked.

"Always."

"Isn't it ironic that we couldn't get along?"

"That's in the past," Marie replied. "We're older now."

"And prayerfully wiser."

"What about my job?" Marie asked. "It tore us apart. You wanted to know what I couldn't tell you. I was sworn to secrecy."

"We'll make it work. God will make it work."

"In the last six years, we've spent so much time separated on two continents." Marie knew he didn't need to be reminded. She wanted to say it anyway, for the record.

"I know, but I'd rather be with you for a few days than without you the rest of my life."

That was some statement, coming from Logan.

"A few days? Is that enough for you?"

"They would have to be." Logan's voice seemed

sure, as though he had made peace with himself and God about how dysfunctional their relationship could be.

"Since we don't know how much time on earth God has given us, let's make the best of the days afforded us," Logan continued. "Marie Bouchard, will you remarry me? Let's start over."

Marie blinked away six years of tears. God had brought them back together again.

Let's start over, he says.

Slowly, she nodded.

"Yes?" Logan asked, as if to confirm their commitment.

"Yes, Logan. Yes." Her hand shook as Logan slid her old engagement ring onto her finger.

It still fit, like it had never left her ring finger.

Her hand was still trembling as Logan held it.

"Your hand didn't shake in Alaska when you knocked that guy out in your stateroom," Logan remarked.

Why did he have to bring it up?

Marie didn't want to pick a fight. She prayed for wisdom. *How do I respond?*

"Well..." Marie stared at the diamond. "That was all head. This is all heart."

"I thank God that He brought you back to me." Logan kissed her hand.

"And you to me." Marie kissed his forehead.

"A little lower, please?" Logan pleaded.

Marie smiled as she pulled him to his feet, and Logan's lips found his match.

"Now I have news of my own," Marie said.

"What?" Logan's eyes were half-closed.

"I quit my job."

"You what?"

"You heard me. I went after Buchanan with Espy. They were going to fire me, so I quit."

"You went after Buchanan? You mean the guy who sent his assassins after us in Alaska?"

Marie nodded. "He's dead. It's over."

"But you lost your job."

"Saved the family."

"What are you going to do now?" Logan sat down on the couch with Marie. "There's plenty of work for freelance translators, I'm sure."

"No need. I already have a new job."

"You do?"

"Yeah."

"Wait. Let me guess. Mendenhall Security."

Marie waited for Logan to calm down. When he looked relaxed, she said, "There's a catch."

Logan threw up his hands. "I knew it."

"It's a desk job, and I'll be in the office five days

a week." Marie waited. "I'll come home on weekends."

"What? Weekends?"

Marie held Logan's hand. "Mendenhall Security is headquartered in the Great Smoky Mountains."

Logan nearly laughed. "You're kidding."

"There's a Mendenhall Resort outside of the little town of Misty Mountain."

"And Esperanza Diaz-Mendenhall is the queen of such a fairytale castle."

Marie laughed. "One of her clients offered to merge with Mendenhall Security, but she won't because she started this company in memory of her husband Lamar."

"I'm sorry. She's widowed."

"For several years now. I was there when— never mind."

"I don't want to know. Why don't they have an office in Atlanta? A branch or something."

"I might actually be doing some work in Alpharetta for one of her biggest clients, who does have an office here."

"Which client, may I ask?"

"I can't say, but they contract for governments."

"How many of those does she have?"

"Several."

"So let me put on my Urquhart Enterprise investor hat for a minute," Logan said. "Espy doesn't want to sell or merge, but she doesn't have the funds to move to a bigger city like Atlanta."

"I don't know the details."

"Atlanta has way better internet connection and infrastructure than small town Misty Mountain."

"That, I concur."

"For you—or anyone else—to get to work fast, you'd have to fly to the Smokies.'"

"Right."

"She could save all that jet fuel and build a clean and green office in, say, Alpharetta or Smyrna or anywhere in metro Atlanta."

"I'm not privy to what's going on at the corporate level, Logan. I'm only a translator."

Logan stared at her, like he was going to say, "Sure."

But he didn't.

"Remember that week we had in Alaska?" Logan asked.

"Uh-huh."

"I was on the phone a lot for several days. I was busy working on some merger talks that Jared came up with, trying to buy a company in England that wanted to expand to the USA."

"I remember."

"Did you know all that fell through?"

"I'm sorry." Marie genuinely was.

"I'm not. As God had worked it out, we now have money to spare. What if Urquhart Enterprises invests in Mendenhall Security, thereby enabling it to build or lease an office in greater Atlanta?"

Marie shook her head. "Don't do it for me."

"It's a win-win. You get to work in Atlanta, and Espy gets to expand her business."

"I don't know. Talk to her."

"I most definitely will..." Logan glanced at the clock. "Right now, we have a more pressing matter."

"What?"

"It's almost noon, and our son's school day is about over. Shall we go together to pick him up?"

Marie's eyes brightened. "Of course!"

Family first.

Or second after God.

But most definitely not before work.

Marie followed Logan out of the house to his pickup truck, the engagement ring still on her finger. The diamond shone in the noonday sun all the way down the road to the kindergarten.

CHAPTER FIFTY-ONE

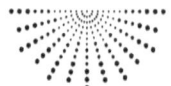

*L*ogan looked in the mirror in the guest bedroom as he adjusted his bow tie. His crisp black tuxedo had no wrinkle on it. His hair was perfectly combed just the way he wanted it.

It was his big day. A bigger day than his first wedding.

At the other end of the house, in a bigger guest bedroom, Marie was getting ready with her matron of honor. They had left their master bedroom alone because that was where they would spend their wedding night after all the guests had gone home.

Esperanza had assured Logan that she wasn't going to let Marie get cold feet. Logan knew that wasn't necessary. He and Marie were meant to be together the rest of their lives.

"You look dashing." Byron Moss walked into the room and sat down in the only armchair there was in the small space. "For a house this large, this room is tiny."

"I know. I don't think we need ten bedrooms. Marie and I have discussed knocking down some of the walls to make the rooms bigger."

"Just don't let the renovation tear you two apart." Byron adjusted his tie. "In fact, don't let anyone tear you apart. Focus on God."

"Did I tell you that your sermon about marriage that Sunday in August hit home?"

"Yes, about a dozen times." Byron looked down at his Bible. "I only preached what God led me to."

Logan turned around. "I think you're one of the best teaching pastors around. I'd hate to see the church move you north to the mountains if they need a pastor there."

Midtown Chapel was determined to raise funds to plant a new church, and had even given it a name: Mountain Chapel. They had scoped out a site in Dahlonega. However, they would only build if they had a hundred percent of the funds.

Logan could write a check, but the church wouldn't let him.

"That's up to God. If He wants me to stay at Midtown, I stay. If He sends me to the mountains, I go. Wherever, God is still with me."

"Right. That's a great attitude."

Byron got up. "In thirty minutes, you'd be married again. I'm going out there to meet some people I've never seen before."

People who would never pass the metal detector test, Logan didn't say.

Mendenhall Security was all over their house. Well, it would be their house again tonight.

Marie had brought nothing with her when she moved back to Atlanta from Paris the day before she came to see him back in August. After their engagement, she moved into a furnished corporate apartment near the newly leased Mendenhall Security branch office in Atlanta. It would only be for two months until the wedding.

Logan asked her to redecorate their house, but she wanted to keep everything the same way they had decorated it after their first wedding. He suspected that she was simply too busy.

My wife was once a bona fide INTERPOL agent who trained with the CIA and MI5 and I can't tell a soul.

On the one hand, Logan was proud of Marie

and her stellar reputation, which Esperanza had alluded to in their corporate investment meetings.

On the other hand, Marie's entire career with INTERPOL was now under seal, and she could never discuss her undercover work and whatever else she did there.

Hunting down Buchanan had killed her career.

But it had saved their family.

And Logan knew then that Marie had always had their family in mind wherever she went.

Now she had come home.

Thank You, Jesus. Thank You. Thank You.

CHAPTER FIFTY-TWO

Surrounded by jewel-toned fall foliage, the Urquhart residence was decorated to the hilt with lace everywhere and pumpkins here and there. They were a somewhat oddball combination, but Jonas wanted pumpkins, and his parents wouldn't deny him that. After all, it was his day too.

Marie knew—and Logan probably did too—that they had spoiled their son by letting him get his way on their second wedding day.

Still, pumpkins and autumn leaves went so well together, both in color and tone, that the wedding planner had agreed to turn the entire wedding into one with a harvest or Thanksgiving motif. She had dyed the lace yellow, red, and orange to match cornucopias and wheelbarrows everywhere.

Marie stood at the guest bedroom window, looking out into the backyard as her matron of honor was getting ready behind her.

There were even haystacks here and there in the backyard. During the wedding planning in September, Marie had expected Jonas to ask for a petting zoo. Sure enough, the boy did.

Logan put his foot down.

"No petting zoo at our wedding," he said firmly to Jonas.

Interestingly enough, Jonas didn't burst into tears. Instead, he pulled an Urquhart. "I'll forego a petting zoo if we get ice cream."

"Forego? Where did you learn that word?" Logan asked.

Marie smiled as she recalled that scene in her mind. Little Jonas possessed some negotiating skills. Either that or he had learned to manipulate his parents.

"I've always loved a fall wedding," Esperanza said from where she was sitting.

The hairstylist was trying to control her wiry hair with more hairspray.

Marie walked back toward her friend. "Thank you for keeping my family safe."

"God did that," Esperanza said.

"Yes, He did. He worked through you."

"I'm glad everything ended well." Esperanza frowned in the mirror when the hairstylist worked a few pins into her hair. "Maybe we should just let my hair be."

"It'll look better in a minute..."

"I've had this hair for forty years. I don't think *better* is what I want to hear."

"Take the pins out," Marie said to the hairstylist. "She can have whatever hair she wants. I don't want anyone in my bridal party to be uncomfortable at my wedding."

"Thank you," Esperanza said.

"But there's no need for you to carry that." Marie pointed to the concealed holster that Esperanza had somehow managed to stuff into her bodice.

Esperanza frowned.

"Your men and women are all over the place. You've trained them well. It will be safe. The wedding ceremony itself is only forty minutes long."

"Anything can happen in forty minutes."

"Well, we'll have to pray and trust God to keep us safe for forty minutes," Marie said. "After all, He's the one who can keep us safe for our entire lifetime, many minutes over."

Pray and trust God.

Marie repeated it quietly to herself as she spoke with Esperanza in their bridal room, and minutes later, all the way down the stairs to the terrace leading to the garden arch, where Logan stood with his best man, his cousin Jared, and Pastor Byron Moss from Midtown Chapel.

The beautiful medley of old hymns that accompanied the bridal procession across the lawn made Marie praise God and desperate to sing along. The small orchestra from Midtown Chapel had played at weddings many times, but this medley was a special arrangement that Marie and Logan had commissioned.

Marie held on to her father's arm for support. This was the second time Father was giving her away—to the same man.

Behind Marie, an unarmed Esperanza held the hem of her ivory train.

Marie smiled when her eyes met Logan's. When Father handed Marie to Logan, she saw the tears in Logan's eyes.

There were no longer any unsealed secrets between Marie and Logan. She had told him what she did for INTERPOL all those years. As much as she could, anyway. He had taken it surprisingly well, and was especially pleased that she had not killed anyone—to her knowledge.

He joked that he didn't want to marry or remarry a killer.

Marie explained that for the most part, she simply translated. Sometimes she was required to go undercover, and that was part of the job.

She didn't tell him that the dangers had only increased exponentially since the FBI and then, Esperanza, got into the arena.

Otherwise she led a lackluster life on the job.

Ironically, since the formation of Mendenhall Security, with well-defined roles within legal boundaries, Marie's new job saw her sitting at the desk most of the time, translating back and forth in several languages. The rest of the time, she filed reports.

And she loved it.

Because she could go home at the end of the day to her soon-to-be husband again and their son.

Marie and Logan chose to repeat the same vows they had before. This time they meant it with all their hearts.

From this day forward, they would be transparent with each other. In fact, they had started to be honest with each other since the day of their engagement in August, when Marie had told Logan everything she could, including the fact that she had worked for INTERPOL throughout their entire marriage, but due to the nature of her assignments, she had to keep Logan in the dark for his own safety and that of their only son.

Esperanza had come in later to fill in the rest of the information that Marie couldn't talk about—after Logan signed a confidentiality agreement to allow his company to invest in Mendenhall Security.

The wedding ceremony almost hit a snag when the ring-bearer could not be found.

Marie and Logan looked at each other, alarmed.

Where is Jonas?

"He was here a minute ago," the wedding planner said. Her face was bright red.

Marie scanned every row to see if Jonas might be sitting with his friends. She couldn't see him anywhere.

Mrs. Ping left her captain at his seat and halfway ran across the lawn back to the house, followed by half of Mendenhall Security on duty.

They've lost my son.

Marie nearly stepped off the platform to go after them.

Logan held her back.

"I'll go." Esperanza kicked off her heels and bolted down the aisle barefooted.

The orchestra began playing a soft melody as time stood still.

Marie leaned toward Pastor Moss and whispered something in his ear.

He nodded. Flipped through his Bible and began reading Ephesians 5. When he reached the twenty-eighth verse, Jonas—and the wedding bands —still hadn't appeared.

"'So ought men to love their wives as their own bodies. He that loveth his wife loveth himself.'" And he kept reading.

Marie prayed silently like she had never prayed before.

"We can still be married without the wedding bands," Logan whispered in her ear. "Our marriage depends on God, not manmade rings."

Marie nodded.

When Pastor Moss reached the end of the chapter, he kept reading. "Ephesians 6:1-3, ladies and gentlemen."

Children, obey your parents
in the Lord, for this is
right. "Honor your
father and mother,"
which is the first
commandment with

promise: "that it may be
well with you and you
may live long on the
earth."

The crowd chuckled.

Marie spotted one of the Mendenhall guards carrying Jonas in his arms, as though he were a football. Esperanza was running behind him. Mrs. Ping stopped to catch her breath.

"Mommy!" Jonas was screaming.

Behind Marie and Logan, Pastor Moss was still reading. "Hear this, everyone. 'And you, fathers, do not provoke your children to wrath, but bring them up in the training and admonition of the Lord.' Ephesians 6:4. Do I get an amen?"

"Amen!"

As Marie watched Jonas approach her, she saw that there were stains all over his black tuxedo. They were in all colors of...

Ice cream.

Remain calm.

No need to panic.

This is only a wedding.

We have a lifetime ahead of us.

The security guard put Jonas down on the grass, and shook off the ice cream on his hands and sleeves. There was ice cream on his hair and face as well, but nobody dared to point it out.

Esperanza's hair was all over the place, like a bunch of springs that went this way and that. Marie regretted telling the hairstylist to remove the pins.

Esperanza held the two wedding bands in her hand, but hesitated to give them to Jonas.

Sticky fingers?

Here came Mrs. Ping, with hand wipes. *What a dear!*

In front of everyone, and as though it were all part of the process, Mrs. Ping gently wiped ice cream off Jonas's face and hands.

Then she took the two rings from Esperanza and handed them back to Jonas. "Now give them to your mommy and daddy when the pastor says so, okay?"

Jonas nodded.

Mrs. Ping didn't return to her seat. She stood next to Jonas, just in case. For that, Marie was appreciative.

The ring exchange ceremony went without a hitch, even with an added lemony scent from the antibacterial hand wipes.

"I now pronounce you husband and wife," Pastor Moss said. "Again."

The entire crowd cheered and clapped.

"You may kiss the bride," he told Logan, who promptly discharged his first duties as a newly re-minted husband.

Again.

They stepped down the platform hand in hand. Logan scooped up Jonas and let him ride on his shoulders, smearing ice cream all over his tuxedo.

Logan didn't seem to mind, and neither did Marie.

She loved that man for putting his difficult son above etiquette and decorum—even though they'd have to discuss later how to teach some common sense into their five-year-old.

It was pointless for Marie to say that she hadn't been like that at that age. She wasn't Jonas.

It was also irrelevant at this moment to say that if their marriage hadn't broken up, Jonas wouldn't be like this or that.

The wedding was a new beginning for their family. To start over. To start fresh again. For that, Marie was grateful to God.

From this day forward...

Marie smiled and waved to everyone as they walked down the aisle back toward the house, as if it was the most natural thing for wedding gowns and bridegroom tuxedos to be smeared with multiple flavors of ice cream. On camera, to boot.

When they reached the house, they would change into clean clothes. Maybe Jonas could take a quick shower.

And no ice cream for him for at least a week. Or two. Or a month!

Marie chuckled.

"What's so funny?" Logan asked. "You don't like strawberry and chocolate flavors?"

Marie didn't say anything.

"I'm sorry, Mommy," Jonas said. "I won't do it again."

"There won't be another time, Son," Logan said. "This is our last wedding and we're married for life, aren't we, love?"

"Absolutely," Marie replied.

"Jonas, I'm going to put you down now because I'm going to kiss your mommy." Logan squatted down and Jonas climbed off.

"Can I watch?" Jonas asked.

"You only do this to the only woman you ever love whom you want to spend the rest of your life with." Logan gently pulled Marie toward him.

She lifted up her chin toward him, waiting to see what he was going to demonstrate to their son.

Logan sure took his time, moving his lips from her forehead to her cheek and then her chin before he reached her waiting—craving—lips.

He didn't disappoint.

It was more than what Marie had expected. And she knew he meant to tell her that there would be more of these kisses to come for the rest of their lives together as husband and wife.

Many, many more.

DEAR READER:

Thank you for reading *Wait for Me*. I hope you enjoyed the novel about Logan and Marie's family sailing to new beginnings. The next novel in the series, *Look for Me*, is another second chance romance with a side of suspense as well, but this time, the story is set on land in the beach town of Key Largo, Florida. Remember Martin McFarland from *Smile for Me*? In *Look for Me*, he has moved on from motorcycles to muscle cars. Now that life is looking great, he wants to start a family, but the only woman he has ever loved is gone. Or is she?

Look for Me (Vacation Sweethearts Book 4)
JanThompson.com/look

Did you enjoy the suspense side of *Wait for*

Me? You might recall that Esperanza Diaz-Mendenhall appears in the previous novel, *Reach for Me*. That book takes place before Mendenhall Security is formed. Esperanza will appear again in *Once a Hero* (Protector Sweethearts Book 2) and *Once a Spy* (Protector Sweethearts Book 3) and then in a new future series she leads.

Reach for Me (Vacation Sweethearts Book 2):
JanThompson.com/reach

Once a Hero (Protector Sweethearts Book 2)
JanThompson.com/hero

Once a Spy (Protector Sweethearts Book 3)
JanThompson.com/spy

Back to the Vacation Sweethearts series, read on for a sneak peek of the next novel, *Look For Me...*

THE NEXT NOVEL IS LOOK FOR ME

VACATION SWEETHEARTS BOOK 4

She needs a champion. Just not him.

Four years after his girlfriend ghosted him, Martin MacFarland finds her in south Florida—abused, pregnant with her second child, and in danger.

Martin wants to be there for her, but she can't give him a second chance.

Remember the MacFarlands in *Smile for Me* (Vacation Sweethearts Book 1)? *Look for Me* is the story of Tina's brother, Martin. We visit the southern coast of Florida, where Martin MacFarland goes to find his long-lost ex-girlfriend.

This Christian beach town romance novel with a side of suspense has clean language while dealing with the difficulties of past sins, single motherhood, second chances, redemption, and the mercy of God.

SHE NEEDS A CHAMPION...

A single mother on the run, Corinne Anderson has made many mistakes since she broke up with Martin MacFarland four years ago. Each mistake compounds on the other problems in her life.

Down and out, Corinne and her three-year-old daughter end up in the small beach town of Key Largo, hiding from the criminals looking for them. When their witness protection cover is blown, Corinne needs all the help she can get to stay safe.

As long as it's not from Martin.

ANYONE BUT HIM...

After his father gives him half the ownership of the MacMuscles Classic Car Restoration business in Savannah, Georgia, Martin MacFarland is convinced that he is ready to settle down and start a family. Unfortunately for him, the only woman he ever loved has vanished without a trace.

After his private investigator tracks her down, Martin drives to Key Largo, praying that Corinne will forgive him for what he did before he became a Christian, and hoping she might consider starting over with him.

Well, she can't. And she won't tell him why either.

YET HE WON'T LEAVE...

As Martin gets closer to finding out what Corinne is up to or hiding from, will he fall into the same fire that has burned Corinne so many times? Will his love survive the flames?

Look for Me is Book 4 in *USA Today* bestselling author Jan Thompson's **Vacation Sweethearts** collection of contemporary Christian travel romance novels celebrating the immeasurable grace and undeserved mercy of God. These **Vacation Sweethearts** novels are a spin-off of Jan's inspirational **Savannah Sweethearts** series. Some of the novels in **Vacation Sweethearts** are also a prelude to the **Protector Sweethearts** Christian romantic suspense series.

Look for Me (Vacation Sweethearts Book 4)
JanThompson.com/look

Vacation Sweethearts
JanThompson.com/vacation

Jan Thompson's Book News Mailing List:
JanThompson.com/newsletter

LOOK FOR ME CHAPTER 1
SNEAK PEEK

VACATION SWEETHEARTS BOOK 4

Martin MacFarland parked his bright tangerine 1966 Shelby GT350 in the last spot by the curb. He lifted his sunglasses to take a clearer look across the small street.

On a sidewalk bench in front of the Key Largo Chocolate Shop, a woman wearing a bright orange apron—that matched the colors of the sign above the windows behind her—was eating her sandwich the way his ex-girlfriend would—all around the edges first. Martin remembered teasing her about her eccentricities when they had both worked at his sister's pottery studio, she as the office manager and he as his sister's personal assistant.

Could that be Corinne Anderson?

Except for her long hair—in a new honey blonde color and tied back in a ponytail—she didn't look much different from the last time Martin had seen her two days after his sister's wedding four years before.

Had it been that long?

The August sunshine swept across the treeless Florida road, casting a bright spotlight on the woman seated on the bench. The more Martin stared, the more confident he was that she was Corinne.

I should never have let her go.

He hadn't forgotten her after she ghosted him as soon as they broke up four years ago, but it wasn't until he'd had a string of failed relationships for the next three years that he realized what he had missed.

Now that he was an income-producing co-owner of MacMuscles Classic Car Restoration, he could afford to settle down—with the right woman.

His sister Tina reminded him that Corinne hadn't shown signs of being a Christian when she walked out of his life. Today, she might still be unsaved. If so, her worldview would be different from Martin's. He had to keep in mind who would raise his future children.

Would the mother of his kids be willing to take them to a Christian church if she didn't believe in God or Jesus Christ?

Nonetheless, Martin had to find Corinne. Whether she was a believer or not, Martin wanted to ask her forgiveness for stringing her along and then trying to marry her when he felt guilty about their intimate relationship.

It had taken Martin one more year to track her down, with most of the work done by his private investigator friend, Ming Wei, who had connections all over North America.

Corinne Anderson was Dinah Miller now, but the records showed she wasn't married.

The reason she was living under an assumed name was anybody's guess. Why did she change her name? Why was she hiding from the world?

And from me, perhaps?

Well, Martin figured she must not be in too

much danger—because she only ran as far away as Key Largo, Florida.

He could make the drive in eight hours if he drove straight through—nine, if he stopped to refill the gas tank and get food.

No, he didn't have to ask Ming for permission—even though Ming had specifically told him that he didn't have more information beyond the chocolate shop. The private investigator was working on something, but he wouldn't know what to tell Martin until Monday.

Monday!

After a restless four or five hours of sleep, Martin was wide awake at two o'clock on Thursday morning. Staring at the ceiling, he made a snap decision to go. He hurriedly packed up a small overnight bag, and he was on the road in thirty minutes, reaching Key Largo at 11:30 a.m., stopping at a fast food drive through along the way.

Fifteen minutes later, there she was. On the bench, under the sun.

As clear as day, that was Corinne.

Martin unbuckled his safety belt, but didn't leave the driver's seat. He drank the remaining lukewarm coffee from a late breakfast as his eyes fixed upon Corinne, aka Dinah, who had finished her lunch.

Martin rolled down his window. The blast of hot Florida air slapped away the cool air inside his car. It must be at least ninety degrees.

It was then that it felt odd to Martin that Corinne was wearing such oversized long-sleeved shirt and baggy pants.

As long as Martin had known her, she was the spaghetti-strap type of girl, going to work at Tina's office in sleeveless blouses whenever she could, even if the air-conditioner was on full blast in the pottery studio.

However, four years later in subtropical Florida —with a late summer even hotter than coastal Georgia—Corinne was wearing such shapeless clothes. Why?

He wanted a closer look.

Martin watched her enter the chocolate shop. He rolled up his window. Time to confront her, to see if she still remembered him—or cared to remember him.

How do I approach her?

Martin prayed to God for wisdom. He had been saved for only four years and his prayers were not yet as strong or clear as his sister's or his brother-in-law's, who was now the assistant pastor at a church in metro Atlanta.

However, Pastor Flores from Martin's own

church said that God would hear the prayers of his heart even if he couldn't form the words. As he learned to pray more, he would have more words to pray.

Martin willed his heart to speak to God, though he could not come up with anything concrete or specific. Perhaps the coffee had spiked his system to the point of making him jittery. Perhaps the drive from Savannah had sapped his strength. Whatever it was, he couldn't find the words.

Finally, he bleated a weak, "Read my heart, Lord Jesus."

It would have to do. Otherwise he might as well go home.

His only purpose of coming down to this small beach town was to get a glimpse of the only woman he truly loved.

Now he must talk to her, to see if she was real, that she wasn't a doppelgänger. To see if she still remembered him. If there was still any hope for them.

And if she had met Jesus since their sad parting.

No doubt it would be a difficult conversation. Their breakup had been anything but sweet. On the day before Tina's wedding, Martin had accepted Jesus Christ as his personal Lord and

Savior, thereby making him a brand-new man who wouldn't sleep with Corinne any more until their wedding night.

"I don't want to marry you!" Those were her last words as she threw his apartment keys at him— leaving a small scar on his cheek—and walked out into the streets of Savannah in the pouring evening rain.

The next day, she quit her job at Tina's Turn Pottery Studio, moved out of her house, sold her car, changed her phone number, cut off all contacts with her friends and relatives, and disappeared from Martin's world.

Until now.

Look for Me (Vacation Sweethearts Book 4)
JanThompson.com/look

More Information about Vacation Sweethearts:
JanThompson.com/vacation

Subscribe to Jan's book news mailing list:
JanThompson.com/newsletter

ACKNOWLEDGEMENTS

Many thanks to my Georgia Press publishing team for keeping up with my writing schedule.

With God-given eyes for copyediting details, Lenda Selph is my patient copyeditor and proofreader for this novel. I appreciate her and thank God for her invaluable hard work. For additional proofreading, I thank copyeditor Lesley McDaniel and proofreader Kim Kemery.

I am grateful to God for my husband and son for their support and encouragement.

And I'll always remember my beloved mother and my late father for having instilled in me the love of reading and writing from a very early age. I miss my father here on earth, but I will see him in heaven some bright day.

Most of all, I am eternally thankful to my Lord and Savior, Jesus Christ, who died on the cross to save me from my sins and rose again from the grave to give me eternal life. Without Him, I can write and do nothing.

Jan Thompson
John 3:16

BOOKS BY JAN THOMPSON

CHRISTIAN ROMANTIC SUSPENSE & BEACH ROMANCE

BINARY HACKERS (NEAR-FUTURE INSPIRATIONAL ROMANTIC THRILLERS)

- Book 1: Zero Sum
- Book 2: Zero Day
- Book 3: Zero Base
- Book 4: Zero Trust

PROTECTOR SWEETHEARTS (CHRISTIAN ROMANTIC SUSPENSE)

- Book 1: Once a Thief
- Book 2: Once a Hero

- Book 3: Once a Spy
- Book 4: Twice a Fighter
- Book 5: Twice a Convict
- Book 6: Twice a Soldier

DEFENDER SWEETHEARTS (CHRISTIAN ROMANTIC SUSPENSE)

- Book 1: Never a Traitor
- Book 2: Never a Hostage
- Book 3: Never a Fugitive
- Book 4: Always a Maverick
- Book 5: Always a Champion
- Book 6: Always a Guardian

SAVANNAH SWEETHEARTS (CHRISTIAN COASTAL CITY & BEACH TOWN ROMANCE)

- Prequel: Ask You Later
- Book 1: Know You More
- Book 2: Tell You Soon (Romance with Suspense)
- Book 3: Draw You Near
- Book 4: Cherish You So
- Book 5: Walk You There

- Book 6: Love You Always (Romance with Suspense)
- Book 7: Kiss You Now
- Book 8: Find You Again
- Book 9: Wish You Joy (Christmas Year Round)
- Book 10: Call You Home

VACATION SWEETHEARTS (CHRISTIAN TRAVEL ROMANCE)

- Book 1: Smile for Me
- Book 2: Reach for Me (Romance with Suspense)
- Book 3: Wait for Me (Romance with Suspense)
- Book 4: Look for Me (Romance with Suspense)
- Book 5: Pray for Me
- Book 6: Care for Me
- Book 7: Cheer for Me

SEASIDE CHAPEL (CHRISTIAN SMALL
TOWN BEACH ROMANCE)

- Book 1: His Longing Heart (second edition of Share with Me)
- Book 2: His Wake-Up Call (second edition of Step with Me)
- Book 3: His Morning Kiss (previously published as Sing with Me)
- Book 4: His Quiet Serenade
- Book 5: His Waiting Love
- Book 6: His Beach Retreat

Subscribe to Jan Thompson's mailing list:
JanThompson.com/newsletter

SEASIDE CHAPEL

Welcome to *USA Today* bestselling author Jan Thompson's Seaside Chapel Christian beach romance series. These novels are set on real-life St. Simon's Island, Georgia—a beach town where history is all around and the future is a moment away—and the neighboring fictitious Seaside Island, where the rich and famous live.

Savor the small-town atmosphere and the warm southern beaches of St. Simon's Island and the idyllic Golden Isles along the Atlantic Ocean. Enjoy the music of the orchestra and hymns of the church, and hang out with our Christian friends who attend Seaside Chapel, a little church by the sea known for its beach weddings and fair share of love and life.

As these Christians grow in their knowledge and understanding of God, they are tested in their spiritual maturity, their love lives, and their relationships with others. Share their heartaches and healing, and cheer them on as they celebrate faith, family, and friends.

JanThompson.com/seaside

- Book 1: His Longing Heart (second edition of Share with Me)
- Book 2: His Wake-Up Call (second edition of Step with Me)
- Book 3: His Morning Kiss (previously published as Sing with Me)
- Book 4: His Quiet Serenade
- Book 5: His Waiting Love
- Book 6: His Beach Retreat

SAVANNAH SWEETHEARTS

Welcome to the new south! From *USA Today* bestselling author Jan Thompson come these clean and wholesome, sweet and inspirational Christian romances set on the romantic beaches of Tybee Island and in the coastal town of Savannah, Georgia.

Meet a group of multiracial and multiethnic churchgoing Christians who love the Lord, work hard in their careers, and seek God's will for their love lives. Against a backdrop of ocean, sand, and sun, these inspirational romances showcase aspects of the human need for God and for one another. Have some tea, settle in a comfortable reading chair, and enjoy these sweet celebrations of faith, hope, and love in Jesus Christ.

JanThompson.com/savannah

- Prequel: Ask You Later
- Book 1: Know You More
- Book 2: Tell You Soon (Romance with Suspense)
- Book 3: Draw You Near
- Book 4: Cherish You So
- Book 5: Walk You There
- Book 6: Love You Always (Romance with Suspense)
- Book 7: Kiss You Now
- Book 8: Find You Again
- Book 9: Wish You Joy (Christmas Year Round)
- Book 10: Call You Home

VACATION SWEETHEARTS

Travel with our friends from Savannah, Georgia, to the coast and to the mountains. Cheer them on as they celebrate the immeasurable grace and undeserved mercy of God through Jesus Christ.

The Vacation Sweethearts novels are a spin-off of Jan's Savannah Sweethearts series, and fans will recognize familiar faces from Riverside Chapel, a church in the coastal city of Savannah, Georgia. In fact, we might even visit the beach town of Tybee Island from time to time to visit old friends and beloved families...

JanThompson.com/vacation

- Book o (Prequel): Time for Me
- Book 1: Smile for Me (International Romance)
- Book 2: Reach for Me (Romance with Suspense)
- Book 3: Wait for Me (Romance with Suspense)
- Book 4: Look for Me (Romance with Suspense)
- Book 5: Pray for Me (International Romance)
- Book 6: Care for Me
- Book 7: Cheer for Me (International Romance)

PROTECTOR SWEETHEARTS

Private investigator Helen Hu and her associates specialize in searching for missing persons and hunting for lost treasures. Join them in their adventure suspense around the world in *USA Today* bestselling author Jan Thompson's Protector Sweethearts, a series of Christian Romantic Suspense with a side of mystery. Protector Sweethearts is a spin-off of Savannah Sweethearts and Vacation Sweethearts.

∾

JanThompson.com/protector

- Book 1: Once a Thief

- Book 2: Once a Hero
- Book 3: Once a Spy
- Book 4: Twice a Fighter
- Book 5: Twice a Convict
- Book 6: Twice a Soldier

DEFENDER SWEETHEARTS

Defender Sweethearts is a sister series to the Protector Sweethearts Christian romantic suspense collection. While the heroes in Protector Sweethearts search for lost treasures and lost people, the Defender Sweethearts novels focus on protecting the helpless and hopeless. The main characters in Defender Sweethearts come from the supporting cast in Protector Sweethearts.

JanThompson.com/defender

- Book 1: Never a Traitor

- Book 2: Never a Hostage
- Book 3: Never a Fugitive
- Book 4: Always a Maverick
- Book 5: Always a Champion
- Book 6: Always a Guardian

BINARY HACKERS

Like more suspense with your Christian romance? Like to read suspense thrillers? If you're looking for clean near-future romantic suspense without compromising the Christian faith, these books are for you.

From *USA Today* bestselling author Jan Thompson come these inspirational near-future cyberthrillers combining technothriller and romance, starting with Binary Hackers that feature computer specialists living at the edge of cyberspace, where they have to juggle being law-abiding truth-telling Christians while carrying out their assignments by any and all means possible.

The Binary Hackers series is set in the same story world as Jan's other books, and characters from the other series may make cameo appearances in this series and vice versa.

JanThompson.com/binary

- Book 1: Zero Sum
- Book 2: Zero Day
- Book 3: Zero Base

ABOUT JAN THOMPSON

USA Today bestselling author Jan Thompson writes clean and wholesome contemporary Christian romance with elements of women's fiction, Christian romantic suspense with an air of mystery, and inspirational international thrillers with threads of sweet Christian romance. Jan's books are for readers who love inspiring stories of faith, hope, and love in Jesus Christ.

Raised on a tropical island in the eastern hemisphere, Jan now lives and writes in the western hemisphere. Her international background gives her a unique multicultural and multiracial perspective to her novels and books. The island has never left her, and she reminisces about beach life in her beach romance novels.

When Jan is not busy writing small-town stories, she writes big-city romantic suspense and international technothrillers, a nod to her previous career in computer science. She weaves technology with human interests, reflecting the current and future digital world. And romance. There's always romance.

Beyond the printed page, Jan is a wife, mother, family scribe, avid reader, occasional artist, erstwhile pianist, and chief of staff to the family cat.

For God so loved the world,
that He gave His only begotten Son,
that whosoever believeth in Him
should not perish,
but have everlasting life.
—John 3:16